A Jester for Ellie

A Jester for Ellie

ANTON BUDISIN

gatekeeper press

Columbus, Ohio

A JESTER FOR ELLIE

Published by Gatekeeper Press
2167 Stringtown Rd, Suite 109
Columbus, OH 43123-2989
www.GatekeeperPress.com

Library of Congress Control Number: 2022941166

ISBN (paperback): 9781662929830
eISBN: 9781662931574

*I wish to dedicate this book
to my wife, Marion
Without her daily support, I would not have been able
to find the confidence and courage
to finally complete this story.*

The weather forecast for that afternoon called for rain and strong winds; the overcast lack of sunshine seemed to promise a February storm. Dane was on the neighboring roof, nailing a patch of shingles over a small gap. Ellie had been watching him work on his house for the past two weeks, always wanting to approach him but always shying away. On this day, she decided, she would finally find a plausible reason to meet him. She had begun watching him when he had first begun working that day, observing in anticipation as he cleaned out the gutter of leaves and dirt. *No, not time yet…relax,* she thought to herself.

He climbed the last steps of the ladder to get on top of the roof. After thinking a second, he descended, went inside, and returned with a hammer, nails and box of tiles. Now seemed to be the perfect time to run across and greet him. She had gotten up her nerve and begun to walk quickly, but after a few steps her phone rang. She ran inside to answer it. Wrong number. By the time she was outside again, he was already on the roof. *He's probably going to be up there all day*, she thought. *Okay, Ellie, this is it. Let's do it. It's now or never.*

While she was approaching the house, she began to evaluate his situation. *He seems nice. I wonder if he's got a girlfriend. I haven't seen a wife or a steady live-in. Maybe he's gay. I bet he's weird.*

Stop making excuses. Let's get it over with now.

Perhaps it might be better to wait 'til after it rains.

No! NOW!

Another call from below startled him. The hammer slipped from his hand, bounced off the roof, fell into a box of bottles, and shattered the contents inside. Turning around and looking down, he saw her standing there. She was biting her finger while looking up at him. She was covered with grease… arms, hands, face, hair and clothes. After staring at her for a few seconds, he turned his gaze to the box of broken bottles.

Ellie: I'm really sorry if I startled you. And I'm sorry I made you drop your hammer and break those bottles.

She tried to hide a laugh, but a few giggles escaped.

Dane: [A bit sarcastically] Well, I suppose I didn't really need to drink all that wine anyway.

Ellie: I'll gladly replace them. It was my fault.

Dane: Don't worry about it. Did you want me for something?

Ellie: Well, yes. If you can spare a minute.

She was getting nervous. He didn't seem as friendly as she had hoped.

Dane: I don't mean to be rude, but I'm kind of busy at the moment.

Ellie: I'm sorry. Fine. I'm sorry to have bothered you. [Beginning to walk away] But I do intend to replace the wine.

Dane: Okay. Okay. Just hang on a minute. I'm coming down. I've got to pick up the hammer anyway.

He starts coming down.

> Ellie: I've got your hammer.
>
> Dane: Alright. Hold on a second.
>
> Ellie: Thank you so much. I promise it'll only take a few minutes.
>
> Dane thought to himself, *Sure, now it's turned into a few minutes. What next, a half-hour? She does seem to be awfully cute beneath all that grease and grime, though.*

While he had been considering her appearance, he lost his concentration, lost his grip, and proceeded to fall a few steps. He tried feverishly to get a grasp on the ladder and, finally doing so, he found himself dangling as his feet swung freely below him. He soon got a footing and cautiously continued to the ground below. Once upon the ground, he turned to face the young lady and observed that she was laughing.

Ellie: I'm sorry for laughing…you're quite a funny guy. [Now holding back her laughing] Are you alright?

Dane: [Smirking, embarrassed] Oh, just wonderful. Wait until you see my closing act.

She handed him the hammer, then gestured at herself.

Ellie: Ellie.

Dane: Bozo.

Ellie: [In disbelief] No.

Dane: Actually, Dane.

Ellie: Glad to meet you, Dane.

Dane: Same here. But honestly, before it begins to rain, I've got to nail those shingles on the roof before I have a flood. [Puts out hand and feels for rain]
Nope. Too late. It's beginning to drizzle already.

Ellie didn't want to make things worse, so she decided to speed things up a bit.

Ellie: It's my Bimmer. It won't start.

Dane: Your Bimmer? What the hell is a…

Ellie: A BMW.

Dane: Great. Another yuppie neighborhood. Just what I need. Well, there's only one problem. You see, you've neglected to ask me a very important question.

Ellie: What's the question?

Dane: You didn't ask me if I knew anything about foreign cars.

Ellie: Does it really matter? What a jerk I am. I blew it.

Dane: [Giving a smile] Well, let's have a look, anyway.

Ellie: Gee, thanks. I really appreciate it.

Ellie gave her first genuine smile of the day. She pointed out the Bimmer, as she called it, and they proceeded towards it. Upon reaching the car, Dane peered into the engine. Ellie began to look him over. He was slender but well-built, she noticed. His arms showed a well-formed contour of muscles.

Dane: [Still under the hood] . . . Does it?

Ellie: What? I'm sorry, I didn't hear you.

Dane: I asked you if the radio or horn works. When you tried to…

Ellie honked the horn twice and long. As she did so, Dane jerked his head up and banged his head under the hood.

Dane: Ow! Jesus… [Coming out from under the hood and holding his head] What'd you have to go and do that for?

A JESTER FOR ELLIE

Ellie: Well, you just asked me if the horn worked, so I…

Dane: Yes, but I didn't mean . . . Nevermind. Okay, now we know the horn works, so we can assume it's not the battery…I think.

Ellie: [In low, embarrassed voice] Sorry.

Dane: Don't giggle, alright. Just don't giggle. [Smiling slightly] And please, don't touch the horn, okay?

Ellie: [A bit hurt but still scheming a bit] Fine. You really don't have to be so mean. You looked like such a nice guy, Dane.

Dane: I know. I apologize. I guess you've caught me on a bad day. [Getting under the hood again] Now. Let's see… Maybe…

Ellie: You're a very attractive guy, Dane. [Silence] Come on, Dane, break down and return the compliment.

Dane: Thanks. You too…

Ellie: The name's Ellie, remember?

Dane: Ellie. I was getting to it.

Ellie: Thirty-three?

Dane: Twenty-nine.

Ellie: No, you can't be. You're a thirty-one, minimum.

Dane: Twenty-nine, months ago.

Ellie: [Laughing] Oh, no. I'm talking about your waist.

Dane: My waist? [Still under the hood and half-listening] That's a thirty-two. And I make you out to be a thirty-one.

Ellie: No! You can't be serious.

Dane: I'm referring to your bustline. Ha! I shut her up now.

Ellie: Thirty-four.

Upon hearing that, again Dane jerked his head up and collided with the hood with a loud thump. Ellie was giggling again and heard Dane mumbling between groans.

Dane: I never did like girls who wore heavy sweaters.

Ellie: I heard that. [Still giggling] I have broad shoulders.

Ellie began feeling bad for Dane's vain attempts at fixing the BMW.

Ellie: Listen, Dane, forget about the car. Really. It's beginning to rain hard now, and you still have to finish your roof.

Dane: Just hold on. I think I've almost got it…

Ellie: Really…Don't worry about it anymore. I've decided not to go out in this rain anyway.

Dane: [Now determined] I'm sure I can do something.

Ellie: Before you get a concussion under there.

Dane: What's your rush all of a sudden? At first you wanted me… Come over here and watch.

Ellie got into the car and successfully started the engine.

Dane: Well how do you like that! I've actually fixed the damn Bimmer!

Ellie: What do ya know! You did it. [Looking at him and biting her lip with a look of guilt upon her expression.]

Dane: [Contemplative] Wait a minute.

Ellie took a few steps backwards.

Dane: There wasn't anything wrong with the car in the first place, was there?

Ellie shook her head slowly and gave half a smile.

Dane: You little devil.

He studied her, uncertain how to assess the situation.

Ellie: I only wanted to say hello.

Dane: [Sarcastically] Oh, sure. I couldn't think of any other way of doing that myself. Look at you. You've gotten all greased up to play the role. You should try acting sometime.

Ellie: [In low voice] Are you angry with me?

Dane: I know I should be. In fact, I actually want to be all pissed off with you . . .

Ellie: But you're not! Are you, Dane?

Dane: The least you could do is give me the courtesy of saying that for myself.

Ellie: You're right… Go ahead.

Dane: You're a special one, aren't you.

Ellie: Why, those are the kindest words I've heard from you yet.

Dane: Well, savor them, because they're surely to be the last if I get flooded in my bedroom with all this rain.

Ellie: God! That's right!

Dane: Well, it's been…different…meeting you, Ellie. I know I won't forget it. I really should get back to the roof.

Ellie: [Eagerly] Let me help you. Please, let me.

Dane: And do what? Hold an umbrella?

Ellie: At least that.

Dane: Why don't you go and make something hot, and after I've finished, I'll stop by for a quick one.

Ellie: Wouldn't you like that, Dane. A *quick* one? [Giving him the evil eye]

Dane: You know what I mean. Coffee or tea will be fine.

Ellie: Great. [Looking at him with a sorry expression] Just look at you . . . You're all wet and banged-up because of me.

Dane: Oh, don't worry about me. Just wait until you take a good look at yourself *in* a mirror… you're covered with grease. [Smiling]

A couple of hours later, Dane knocked on Ellie's door. The door opened and Ellie greeted Dane while she stood barefoot in a bathrobe.

Dane: Hello, my name is Bozo.

Ellie: Hi there . . . And I'm Bullwinkle. Glad to meet you.

Dane: May I enter?

Ellie: Surely, after I've validated your passport.

Dane: [Stepping inside, smiling] I see that you've removed the grease.

Ellie: Finally. Sorry I'm not dressed, but I just came out from the shower.

Dane: Quite alright. I've just finished taking mine up on the roof.

Ellie: I would like to formally apologize for earlier… it was very immature.

Dane: [Smirking] That's a good word for it.

Ellie: I deserve that. Let me get dressed and in the meantime you can let it all out.

Dane: Then perhaps I should come back in a few days.

Ellie: [Turning around] What?

Dane: I was only joking . . . Get dressed.

Dane waited in the kitchen, and Ellie returned a few minutes later.

Dane: You sure are pretty, aren't you?

Ellie: [Curiously] Did you ever believe otherwise?

Dane: It's the color of your eyes that really does it to me, you know. They're a radiant silver. The color of the sky just before a spring storm.

Ellie: Don't stop, please continue.

Dane: Do you have any aspirin? I've gotten a terrible headache.

Ellie: Sure. How's your head? It's taken quite a beating.

Dane: Yes, I suppose I could blame that Bimmer of yours. I'll pour the coffee in the meantime.

Ellie: [Returning with aspirin] I should worry about you. First the slip on the ladder, then the hood of the car . . . Not to mention dropping the hammer, which could have killed me. Are you always such a klutz? [Smiling]

Dane: No. Only when I think.

They talked for a long time, drinking a pot of coffee doing so. Ellie was the supervising counselor at a center for abused and handicapped children. She had moved into the neighborhood three years ago, was twenty-seven years old now, had never been married and was presently breaking up with an upcoming "Wall-Streeter" guy, named Jeremy. She had a black and white puppy collie named Missy who was presently sleeping on the couch.

Dane had just moved in two weeks ago from the city, looking for a quiet place to live. He had just quit a well-paying job there because he was getting frustrated and bored with being the buyer of a leading mail-order house. He simply up and left. He would supplement his financial needs by doing carpentry work, a skill he picked up from his father. He also told Ellie he needed time to finish his short stories for a book he was in process of publishing.

Ellie: So that's what you plan to do?

Dane: Yes, as soon as the house is finished. I got a great price because of all the repairs required. Two more weeks should do it, and then off into seclusion I go.

Ellie: Seclusion?

Dane: That's the way I work best when finalizing my writing. I probably won't leave the house for a month or so. You'll know that it's time when you see a large truck pull up my driveway and unload a ton of supplies.

Ellie begins to laugh lightly.

Dane: What's the matter?

Ellie: Nothing… so, I won't see you for a whole month?

Dane: At least that. Anyway, in a few weeks, by the time I'm ready, you'll be sick of me.

I'm not exactly convinced of that, Ellie thought. *If he's trying to get rid of me, he's being very clever about it. He must be a good writer.*

Dane: When do you plan on breaking it off with your boyfriend?

Ellie: When he comes back from Bermuda in two weeks. I
figure he'll be in the best of moods then.

Dane: Sorry for prying, but don't you like Bermuda?

Ellie: Sure I do. But tell my job that.

Dane: Is that really the reason you didn't go?

Ellie: No, I suppose not. It's more like a bunch of guys' idea of a getaway vacation.

Dane: Those bastards. I've heard a lot about those getaway escapes.

Ellie: What about you? Are you trying to escape from anyone? Like me for instance?

Dane: No, not for a long time, the fact being that there hasn't been anyone from whom to escape.

Ellie: [Transparently curious] Oh?

Dane: There's always someone to date when I need.

Ellie: Really?

Dane: No. It's not quite what you're thinking. There hasn't been anyone special for years now. After a few weeks or a month something goes sour, and we both would wish we'd never started anything in the first place.

Ellie: You're better off, believe me.

Dane: [Looking a bit upset and preoccupied] Ellie, it's getting late. I think it's time I got back home.

Ellie: [Backing off too] Fine, I'm kind of tired myself.

Dane: Thank you for everything… honestly. It's been nice meeting you.

Ellie: The same here, Dane. If you ever want to talk again, just knock anytime.

Dane: Maybe I will… good luck with your boyfriend.

Ellie: Thank you.

*   *   *

Days went by, but still no knock on Ellie's door. They would wave to each other occasionally, but there was no physical contact between them. Ellie thought, *If he doesn't want to come over, who cares! He's just another guy.* But later, she would always find herself feeling otherwise. *Okay, so he has no job. That doesn't mean that he's carefree. He's probably a good writer who actually believes in himself. I'm sure he has his reasons… But what's so bad about liking me? He said enough to imply that he's attracted to me. Maybe I've been too forward with him? That's it. No, that's not it. . . I guess time is the only thing I can give a guy like him…*

Ellie continued thinking in a similar fashion for two weeks before she met Dane again in person. It was the second Saturday after their first conversation. Dane was returning home from a hardware store carrying a box of supplies. Ellie's dog, Missy, got loose from her hold and ran towards Dane. Missy jumped up and onto Dane's back, causing him to drop the box. Missy got scared, backed off and sat down. For a second they stared at each other.

Dane: [To dog] You know something, young fella, this neighborhood has a strange and unique way of welcoming new neighbors. So what's your story? Aren't you a cute one. . . Hey, you look familiar. Let's take a look at your nametag. [Reading] Well, what do ya know. Your name seems to be Missy…

Ellie: [Approaching from behind] At least she doesn't bite.

Dane: No, I guess she doesn't… Come over here, Missy. [Smirking] You know, it's not nice to use an innocent puppy like that.

Ellie: That's not fair, Dane. I didn't plan this.

Dane: Alright, alright. I believe you.

Ellie: [Sincerely] Do you really?

Dane: Yes, I do.

Ellie: [Bending over to hug the dog] To think that anyone would let their little dog run across a big street like that just to get a guy's attention. Really!

Missy licked Ellie's nose and barked.

Dane: What? The street isn't exactly a major motorway, lady. I'm sorry, Ellie... so, how have you been?

Ellie: You actually remembered my name.

Dane: I like your name.

Ellie: Have you finished repairing your house?

Dane: After a little cleaning tomorrow, that'll be it.

> Ellie: Oh... That's too bad.
>
> Dane: Why?
>
> Ellie: I don't know. It's just that... Well, hell, I just thought that it would be nice to have gotten together a couple of times before you went into hiding.
>
> Dane: I did mean to call you.

Ellie: You don't need to explain.

Dane: I like you, Ellie. I really do. . .

Ellie: Is it me, Dane?

Dane: No. There's nothing wrong with you. It's me. You seem to be the kind of girl that every man dreams about meeting, but he has to be damn sure that he's ready for you, because if he's not, the whole relationship to follow would be a disaster. That's where I stand right now.

Ellie: Well, being able to just shut off your emotions until you know when the time is right might work for you, but not for me. Maybe, if I was more like you, I could… [Pause] Oh, the hell with it. Thanks for your honesty. I'm sorry about Missy, and I'll make sure she doesn't interfere anymore. You can't blame a girl for trying. [Half-smiling]

Dane: I know I'm going to hate myself for this… We could meet for lunch later, if you like. And I'm not just saying that to be nice.

The hell with him, Ellie. Don't do it. Well, only if you really want to. You're such a jellyfish, Ellie!

Dane: You have a way about you… You've got a knack of making someone feel important.

Ellie: Perhaps you are important. I wish I had a chance to find out. But I'll take what I can get at the present time. Why don't you come by a little later?

Dane: We could go out to eat if you prefer.

Ellie: Actually, I think it would be nicer having you around the house. God only knows when I'll get another chance like this. Anyway, it would be more casual that way.

Dane: Good. Next time my house will be a little neater, okay?

Ellie: Dane, I hope I haven't been too much of a pain in the ass for you.

Dane: I told you, Ellie, I really do like being with you. I'll see you in a little while.

They had sandwiches and salad for lunch. Dane brought a bottle of wine and a flower from the garden. A great amount of talking took place. Ellie's character and beauty was growing on Dane. He felt it happening and she knew it. She was beginning to feel good about the way things were slowly developing between them. She also felt despair encroaching from within, as she continually reminded herself that he was soon to disappear to finalize his stories.

After they were finished with their food and talk, Dane got up and walked to where Ellie was seated. He bent over and kissed her cheek. She couldn't believe it. Although not much as far as kisses go, it had been Dane's first attempt at romance with her. Ellie loved it, and she couldn't keep herself from blushing.

Ellie: Please don't go, Dane. Please don't hide from me. Kiss me again and again and…

Dane: Ellie? What's the matter?

Ellie: Nothing. I guess I got all caught up in a whirlpool of thought for a second. That's all. I'm looking forward to seeing you again.

Dane: How's tomorrow?

Tomorrow? What's he trying to do to me?

Dane: For a short good-bye.

Ellie: [Tearfully] Dane…

Dane: Oh, please don't do that. God, how I hate it when a girl cries.

Ellie: [Getting up and placing her arms around him] Shut up.

She kissed him on the lips. It was slow, moist and warm. The feeling hit home like a thunderbolt—every muscle in his body began to vibrate, as though he had been thrown on the live rail of a subway train. Ellie took a few steps backwards and gazed at Dane.

Ellie: Now that that's out of my system, you can leave. [Teary] It's really up to you from this point on. I don't know what else to do or say to you.

Dane: You're doing fine. [In a serious tone] You don't know what you're getting into.

Ellie: You just let me worry about what's good and bad for me.

Dane: I've got to go… I'll come by tomorrow before I start writing.

Ellie: Okay.

As Dane was walking home he reminded himself that he shouldn't get involved, but his defenses were growing weaker by the minute.

*   *   *

Sunday morning arrived early for Dane. He was up at six, got dressed and sat outside on the porch. He began staring at Ellie's house and fell deeply into thought. At eight o'clock, while his mind was still wandering, a Jeep pulled up into Ellie's driveway. Dane looked up and watched as a tall, well-built, blonde-haired guy jumped out and proceeded towards Ellie's door. Dane thought, *Typical yuppie Wall-Streeter… It figures.* Dane suddenly remembered that Ellie was planning to break up with her boyfriend that weekend. *Go to it lady. Show him who's boss. What the hell does a girl like her want with a guy like me? Trying to get that square-head preppie jealous, probably. Maybe my perfect escape from her will happen now, when he sweeps her off her feet.* He ran inside so as not to be seen. He knew it would be best not to see her anymore, yet he found himself feeling protective towards her. *Whatever happens, DO NOT GET INVOLVED… Yeah, that's it…*

He was so busy planning he didn't hear Ellie yelling at first. Suddenly, however, the yells grew loud enough to drown out Dane's thoughts. He stepped out the door and looked across towards the two of them and saw that the guy had Ellie by her arms, shaking her violently. He ran across the yard and the street to the driveway.

Dane: Leave her alone!

Jeremy: [Letting go of Ellie] Hey, pal, this is none of your business, so back off!

Dane: You two can yell all you want but lay off of Ellie.

Jeremy: Listen, I'm warning you…

Jeremy had begun to walk towards Dane. Ellie positioned herself between the two of them.

Dane: [Eyes fixed on Jeremy] Get out of the way Ellie, please.

Ellie didn't move.

Dane: I mean it, Ellie. Go inside and get me a beer. This won't take long, trust me.

Ellie ran to the door and then stopped, turned around and watched in terror. A fistfight was inevitable at that point. She knew it; Jeremy knew it; but did Dane know it? *What else am I going to get this poor guy into? He's bigger than Dane. What are you thinking? How are you going to write if he breaks your arm?*

There they stood, Jeremy towering a good three inches above Dane. About a foot apart from touching noses, Jeremy swung at Dane. Dane ducked the blow and retorted with a sweeping right and followed that with a left jab. The first punch landed on Jeremy's jaw while the latter, intended for the stomach, fell short. Jeremy backed away for a few seconds, and then rebounded with a left hook which successfully collided with Dane's stomach. Dane keeled over. Taking a deep breath, he straightened up.

Dane: You son of a bitch… Now I'm the one who's pissed off.

Dane walked up to Jeremy, who had been laughing prematurely. Jeremy took a swing with his right fist and Dane blocked it with his left arm and countered with a right and then a left, each into Jeremy's stomach. The fight ended when Dane followed up with a final up-jab into Jeremy's jaw. Jeremy fell back and down, landing on the lawn. Dane held his right hand in his left and uttered a groan of disgust.

Ellie thought, *He did it… Dane actually did it…*

Dane: Get up, Jeremy… at least, I believe that's your name. Now don't be bashful. Get your ass into that Jeep of yours and drive off. Now.

Jeremy: [Getting up slowly with his hand to his jaw] You're crazy. You can have her, buddy. I hope you both rot together.

Jeremy got into his Jeep and drove away. Dane turned to Ellie and peered into her eyes.

Dane: Are you alright?

Ellie: [Shaking head in disbelief] Yes… What about you?

Dane: Sure, but I think I want that beer about now.

Ellie: How's your stomach?

Dane: A little queasy. But it'll pass. I wasn't going to get involved between you two… but felt I should.

Ellie: I'm glad you did… I've gotten you into so much… [Beginning to cry] Don't tell me to stop crying. I just can't help it… I'll get you that beer.

Ellie ran inside and Dane followed.

Dane: [Trying to cheer her up] It looked like he lost his tan after all that.

Ellie: [Handing Dane a beer] He sure did… Thank you for everything, Dane. And not only for today. You really are a warm, sincere man. I can feel it inside of you. Alive and wanting to come out. And I can feel it fighting to escape. But you won't, or can't, allow that. But, you know, whenever it gets a chance to peek outside of its cell, it lets out a light so radiant that even clouds on a rainy day open up out of…

Dane listened as she spoke. He then walked to her, gazing into her silver eyes. *Those eyes*, he thought. *They're either tear-filled or sparkling. And those words…they're either silly or tranquilizing.* He held her by her waist.

Dane: Cheer up, Ellie. please.

He kissed her briefly on her lips.

Ellie: Not much of a good-bye, is it?

Dane: [Smiling] It's a bit more than I had expected.

Ellie: Listen, you go on home and prepare for your leave of absence. If you don't mind, I'd just like to stop by for a quick second to give you something.

Dane: You really don't have to.

Ellie: I want to. And then, with no hard feelings, I'll leave you alone to complete your book . . . [With false cheer] I will be glad to read it when it's finished.

Dane: Alright… See you later.

Dane left feeling confused yet peaceful. Ellie felt more relaxed than ever concerning her chances with Dane. For whatever reasons he had about not wanting to get involved, she then knew that he did care for her. She also believed that in time, he would open up to her. Lost in her thought, she hadn't noticed that Dane had come back to the door.

Dane: Ellie?

Ellie: [Pleasantly startled] Yes, Dane?

Dane: Do you believe in miracles?

Ellie: [Smiling] Sometimes… Sure.

Dane: That there's a maybe involved in you and I actually being happy together?

Ellie: [Nervously] Yes, Dane . . . I do.

Dane: Good.

He walked away. While deep in thought. Ellie fed Missy and pet her. She thought, *What a wonderful day for fairytales.*

* * *

Later that day, just past three o'clock in the afternoon, with butterflies in her stomach, Ellie proceeded to go to Dane's house. Upon reaching his door, she took a deep breath and knocked.

Ellie: Hello! Dane? Anyone home at the castle?

Dane: [From upstairs] Be right there! If you're a pretty female, you can let yourself inside.

Ellie: So this is your home. [Giggling] Looks pretty damn good for a klutz.

Dane: [Coming down the stairs, smiling] Well, hello there, young maiden. Have you any further battles with dragons for this knight in shining armor?

Ellie: No, my Lordship. All my dragons are of past history. But I come bearing your reward for chivalry.

Dane: What have we here? It feels like a bottle of some sort.

Ellie: I hope you like it. I had no idea what type to pick.

Dane: [Opening the wrapping] Trebbiano! *Bravissimo, mia bella donna!*

Ellie: Do you speak Italian? That was nice.

Dane: A little bit. And this is one of my favorite vinos.

Ellie: Great. I asked the man in the liquor store to choose a wine that a writer would enjoy. He said white is best, because in case it's spilled on paper, you can still read through it. And he picked a dry wine because, and I quote, "Writers tend to be far too fruity to start with."

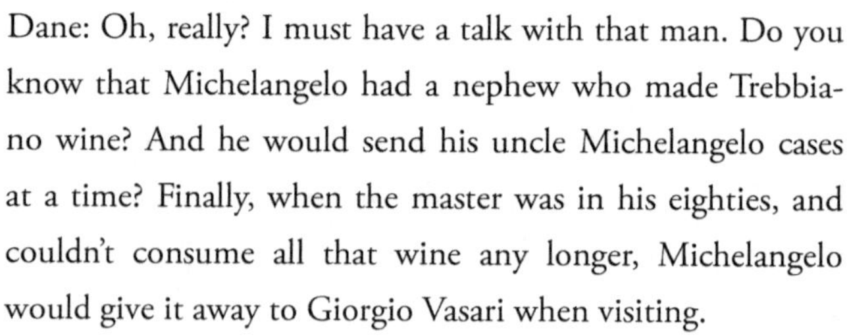

Dane: Oh, really? I must have a talk with that man. Do you know that Michelangelo had a nephew who made Trebbiano wine? And he would send his uncle Michelangelo cases at a time? Finally, when the master was in his eighties, and couldn't consume all that wine any longer, Michelangelo would give it away to Giorgio Vasari when visiting.

Ellie: Vasari... I know that name... Wait a minute. [Thinking] Yes! Vasari wrote *The Lives of the Artists.*

   A JESTER FOR ELLIE

Dane: I'm impressed, Ellie. Really impressed.

Ellie: So this is a bachelor's pad?

Dane: It's more like four pads. I had so much room in need of filling up.

Ellie: [Snooping] After looking at all these boxes of junk, I think you'll have no problem at all.

Dane: Junk? I've come to know all this "junk" as being my closest friends and company, if you don't mind.

Ellie: [Playing along] I'm sorry. Forgive me.

Dane: [Pretending to sulk] Sure, no problem.

Ellie: Honestly, you are the last person I want to fight with.

Dane: [Smiling with curiosity] What's in the other package?

Ellie: Can't wait until Christmas, can you!

Dane: [Trying to peek into bag] I'm not used to receiving gifts.

Ellie: Alright, alright. Go ahead and open it up.

Dane: Can I? Can I really, mommy? Thank you!

Dane shook the box, which was larger than the first and a great deal heavier.

Ellie: [Concerned] Oh, Dane! Please don't shake it!

Dane: I'm sorry. [Opening the box] A corkscrew! I love it!

Ellie: Stop it, silly. See what else is in there.

Dane: Hmm. Heavy and awkward-looking in shape… I know! It's a log! My first log for my first fireplace. I really love this gift—it's the best! Thank you!

Ellie: Will you be a good little boy and open it . . .?

Dane: [Opening the gift] It really does feel like a log…

Upon removing the wrapping of newspaper, he saw a handpainted ceramic caricature of Ernest Hemingway. He kissed it, and then kissed Ellie on her cheek. He was very touched.

Dane: You're batting a thousand. First the trebbiano, and now Hemingway. How did you know?

Ellie: I had a feeling. I'm glad you like it. It's a small way of saying I'm sorry for the car; thank you for the fight, in a crazy sort of way; and…

Dane: You mean there's more to this?

Ellie: Don't interrupt me, I'm on a roll… And finally, it's my way of telling you how new and fresh your moving into this burby neighborhood really is for me. [Pausing] Okay. That's all.

Dane: Let's see. . . You're forgiven; you're welcome; and I'm truly flattered to hear it.

Ellie: Am I being too silly?

Dane: [Sincerely] No, you're not… [Changing tone] Let's open the wine and toast all this. [Picking up the bottle and handing it to Ellie] You open it while I try to dig up some glasses.

Ellie: Let's toast! But you open the wine.

Dane: Why? You deserve to have some fun today.

Ellie: To tell you the truth, I never could discover the secret to opening a bottle with a cork.

Dane: Well, you'd better learn soon, because I like wine.

After finding two glasses, he looked at Ellie. She was sulking a little.

Dane: [Trying not to laugh] What's the matter, mein host?

Ellie: It's not too bad; the cork broke only twice.

Dane: Well let's see. [He looks at the bottle] Fine. Now let me find that strainer. I know it's around here somewhere…

Ellie: No. It can't be that bad…

Dane: I'm only kidding with you.

Ellie: Sure you were. But I told you…

Dane: No, really. . . Now, let's toast. [Pouring the wine and looking at the cork pieces] Looks like you win the toasting honors.

Ellie: Well, then…a toast to Michelangelo, Vasari and Hemingway…may we all aspire to such perfection.

Dane: Brava!

Ellie: Your turn.

Dane: Although highly unconventional… A toast to your liberation from…

Ellie: Jeremy.

Dane: I was getting to it… Jeremy, and to my moving into this "burby" neighborhood and meeting the most clever, devious, adorable and persistent lady I've ever laid eyes upon. [Winking]

Ellie: Thank you…I think.

After the toasts, Dane gave a quick tour of the house. She enjoyed seeing his collectibles and knick-knacks most of all. There were rocks; shells; driftwood; an anchor; old bottles; coins from ancient Rome and Greece; old books; new books; radios from the '40s and '50s; and the list went on.

Ellie: [Amazed] I see now why you required so much space. Dane, you have a museum here.

Dane: Indeed, all this "junk" could fill up a museum in no time at all.

Ellie: I deserve that. I accept your indignation.

Dane: Why don't we finish the wine while sitting on the porch.

Outside, on the porch, they watched the sun as it was beginning to set rather more quickly in the later hours of the day. Again, Ellie was feeling the threat of tomorrow. Dane had obviously postponed his "finalizing" until Monday, and so it was beginning to feel like the end of a newly discovered friendship to her. *I promised Dane not to push it any further*, she thought to herself. *I told him I understood what he had to do and how he had to do it.*

Ellie: So, tomorrow you begin.

Dane: This is the first time anyone or anything has made me postpone my writing. You should be proud.

Ellie: Aren't you the presumptuous type?

Dane: You know I didn't mean it like that.

Ellie: Can't you feel it happening, Dane? Can't you?

Dane: All I can feel right now is the wine, and the sun setting in the sky like a falling giant yellow float.

Ellie: [Pleading] You know you feel more than that. You must feel more than that.

Dane: [Getting upset] Okay, so what if I do? What if I really don't want it? What about my feelings? I very well may just have a good reason.

Ellie: Why can't you tell me? Maybe then I'll be able to better cope with it. Can't you give me that much, if nothing else?

Dane: Last night I began to feel things I know I shouldn't. Then later, when I was all alone again like I'm accustomed to, I got to thinking.

Ellie: [Bitterly] Fine. Don't let me interfere any longer with your loneliness.

Ellie got up from her seat and began to walk away, feeling more angry with herself than with Dane.

Dane: Ellie! Wait! [Sternly] You want it, you've got it. I will fill you in on the personal life of Dane Barringer. Now, sit down and listen. You've very forward with me, so it's time I be upfront with you.

Ellie: [Subdued] Alright. God. I hope this doesn't kill me.

Dane poured himself another glass of wine and began.

Dane: About six years ago, I was involved in a relationship with a girl named Jenny. One fine day Jenny approached me, telling me that she was bearing my child. She was twenty-one and I was twenty-four. After considering all the options, I told Jenny that I would stand by her decision concerning having the baby. I told her that the concept of having a child was wonderful, and that I would want to help her raise it. She insisted upon getting married. I wasn't ready for marriage at the time, but perhaps in time I would've been. Selfishly, I told her that I wanted her to have the baby, but if she chose I would pay for an abortion, but I would not marry her. It was her decision in the end.

At that point, Jenny snapped and became frantic. She screamed that I was a "beast" and a "selfish bastard." She wouldn't hear any more from me or my suggestions. I was young then; perhaps now I would have acted differently, I'm not sure. The same for herself, I assume. She stood up and exclaimed, "To hell with you. I don't want your pity! I'm leaving you! I'm leaving this damn town too! And you will NEVER know my decision. Do you hear me?! You will NEVER know whether or not I decided to keep the baby, or if you have a little boy or girl, alive and breathing the same air that you breathe!"

Then Jenny got up and left. And it was over. I haven't seen or heard from her since. It's been eating at my heart and soul, more so recently than ever before. I haven't been able to reconcile it to this very day. Until then, I feel that any strong relationship must wait.

Dane sat in turmoiled silence. Ellie turned her gaze towards Dane's hands, and saw that they were trembling. Then she noticed blood was dripping from them from the crushing of the glass he had been holding while telling his story. Ellie's pity and self-embarrassment were temporarily cut off by a sense of urgency.

Ellie: [Jumping up] Dear God! Dane, you're bleeding!

Dane: [Mentally still far away] What?

Ellie ran inside and returned with wet towels.

Ellie: Here… Let me see.

She cleaned his hands and wiped away the blood.

Ellie: Cuts on the hands always look worse than they really are. They always bleed a lot more than they should.

Dane: A couple of Band-Aids and I'll be able to write, anyway. Can't seem to do anything one-hundred percent.

Ellie: You should get some rest.

Dane: [Blankly] Right. That's what I need. Lots of time-healing rest.

Ellie: Will you be alright?

Dane: The book's not finished… I have to be alright.

Ellie: [Holding back tears] Well, you'd better get to work on it.

Dane: Thank you.

Ellie: Anytime, Dane.

Not sure what the best thing was to do at that point, Ellie decided to take a chance and leave Dane alone for a while. Later that night, she thought it would be a good idea to go and check on him. She headed towards his house, stopping once to reconsider, and then continued. When she reached his lawn, she could hear an opera playing from inside Dane's house. The music was so breathtaking, she stopped near the porch and sat down upon the steps. Ellie didn't know that it was *La Traviata*; nor did she know that the aria playing was that of the character of Germont trying to ease his son Alfredo's despair over Violetta. The words were foreign to Ellie; however, they pulsated with the harmony and melody of the music. She closed her eyes and listened while the force of the aria carried her far off into the heavens. She could see herself embracing Dane as they danced upon the clouds, caught within the rapture of the serenade. And in the background

Germont sang not to Alfredo, but rather to Dane, pleading with him to find some comfort in his lamentation, asking God to grant Dane peace… *Oh, rammenta per nel duolo, Ch1ivi gioia ate brillo', E che pace cola' sol, ste splendere anchor pio'; Dio mi giudo'! Dio mi giudo'!… Dio mi giudo'!*

The lyrics of the ballad were mesmerizing, soothing, powerful and beautiful. She couldn't recall the last time she had felt so moved. She decided that leaving Dane alone was best. While walking back home. slowly, the magic of the opera played on. Lying in bed that night, she listened as the music radiated from Dane's domain. She fell asleep and found herself in Dane's arms as they sat beneath the shade of a tree while the birds above sang the melodious harmony of the opera.

* * *

It was early Monday morning. Ellie could still hear the opera playing within her mind. She was thinking about Dane and if he had made it through the night alright, when she heard a knock on the door.

Ellie: Hold on a sec.

She opened the door but saw no one. Then she looked down and found a marionette which resembled a clown. Under the doll was an envelope. She carried the two into her house after looking around. She thought to herself, *Dane, what are you up to now?* She opened the envelope and pulled out a card, reading the words "Better to be a court jester and live in bliss // Than be a sage, believing that things get better than this." On the cover of the card was a picture of a clown with a jester's cap, laughing and apparently dancing before a king. Ellie began to smile and looked out her window towards Dane's house. She went to close the door and saw Dane standing there on the porch. She opened her mouth in surprise.

Dane: Hello.

Ellie: You startled me. But it's a wonderful surprise.

Dane: Thank you for yesterday… And not only for the gifts.

Ellie: I should have left you alone. It was none of my business. How's your hand?

Dane: It's just fine. You were right, hands bleed an awful lot.

Ellie: Would you like to come in?

Dane: No. I really just stopped by to say that to you, and to bid a short farewell before I really get into writing.

Ellie: Great. So I guess I won't be seeing you for a while, then.

Dane: [Considerately] Is that alright with you?

Ellie: [Brightly] What? I can't believe it. I mean, of course it is.

Dane: Good. I feel better about it now. Give me a month or so, alright?

Ellie: You never cease to amaze me. I feel good about it now, too.

Dane: Feel free to wave every now and then, okay?

Ellie: [Smiling] You can count on it.

Dane: You'll be honored with getting to read the first finished copy.

Ellie: I can't wait. And we'll celebrate with another bottle of wine. I've been practicing, you know.

Dane: Goodbye, Ellie.

Dane kissed her forehead and hugged her, then turned around and began to walk away.

Ellie: Dane…

Dane: [Turning around] Yes?

Ellie: The opera.

Dane: *La Traviata.*

Ellie: Dio… Gweedo?

Dane: *Dio mi Giud'.* Germont singing to his son Alfredo. You could hear it?

Ellie: Yes. It was beautiful. Thank you.

Dane: [Curiously] You're welcome.

Dane turned and continued home. Ellie stared at him as he walked home.

Later that day, Ellie bought a copy of *La Traviata* and played it in its entirety. She fell in love with Verdi's music as she read along with the libretto. And when Germont sang his lament, she read the words; they were like an omen. "Oh, remember, even in sadness, that joy was yours while there, and that there you may still find peace in the warm sunlight. God grant it! God grant it! God grant it!" Ellie became enchanted and waited for Dane to complete his book. She knew the days would be long, but believed that Dane intended on coming back to her.

*   *   *

Six weeks passed, and Ellie continued to wait and wonder. It was always revitalizing to see Dane outside and wave to him. She often saw him early in the morning outside as she left to go to work; many times, she would see him outside when she returned in the evenings. She often would feel compelled to run to him and say "Hello" or "How's it going?"—but she always held back. The weekends were usually the worst for her. On a few occasions when her friends came to visit, Ellie felt a burning desire to introduce them to Dane; however, again, she did not.

Only once did she find herself almost coming into physical contact with Dane during that time away. Jeremy had come to Ellie's house weeks later. He had demanded that Ellie come out and hear what he had to say to her. Ellie felt apprehensive at the onset, but finally gave in. At one point, Jeremy began yelling, and Ellie instinctively looked across towards Dane's house. And there he was; Dane was standing just inside his doorway. Ellie rediscovered her confidence after seeing Dane. She found herself hoping that Jeremy would start something, but then she began to feel guilty. Ellie yelled a few harsh words of warning that Jeremy should never try to visit again, and Jeremy stormed off and drove away. Feeling good about herself, Ellie turned to face Dane, but he was no longer there. She sighed, turned around, and went back inside.

And now it was April Fools' Day. It was just past three o'clock in the morning. There was a knock upon Ellie's door which sent Ellie turning over to her side. Then there was a second knock. Finally, after the third knock, Ellie awakened and turned on the light in her bedroom.

Ellie: Who the hell *is* that!

There were three more successive raps upon the door. She got up, picked up the metal tube of her vacuum cleaner and cautiously approached the door.

Ellie: [Nervously and cautiously] Who... Who is it?

Dane: A fool with a scroll, fair maiden.

Ellie: [Confused and still sleepy] A fool?

Dane: Yes...with a scroll.

Ellie: [Beginning to wake up] Who the hell...?

Dane: What day is this?

Ellie: March… No… It's April first.

Dane: Correct. And of what other name is this day referred?

Ellie: [Realizing who it is and flinging the door open] April Fools' Day!

There stood Dane, wearing a jester's cap and holding a booklet in his right hand, a bottle of wine with his left.

Ellie: Dane! It's really you!

Dane: You saw through the disguise.

Ellie: Even at three-thirty in the morning, you're still a wonderful sight for sore eyes!

Dane: May I come in? I know you must be sleepy, but . . .

Ellie: Who cares! There's only one condition… If you enter this house at such an ungodly hour, you are not to leave until the sun comes out.

Dane: Uh, oh. [Looking at the booklet] Look at the trouble you've gotten me into now.

Ellie was beginning to tremble inside—butterflies, roller-coasters, the whole bit. She began to hope that the flushing upon her face wasn't obvious, but she couldn't fight her emotions and expectations.

Ellie: Well. What shall it be?

Dane: I suppose you leave me with no other choice…

Ellie's heart began to beat hard.

Ellie: I could just kill you for torturing me like this.

Dane: I guess I'll have to come inside.

Dane stepped inside and extended his arms towards Ellie. They embraced. They clutched one another as if they were holding onto a branch in a river and should they release, they each would surely drown.

Ellie: Oh Dane. I've missed you tremendously. I wasn't sure I could last much longer.

Dane: Shh! I'm back. As I've told you. And these tears of yours…I never really realized just how warm they are until now.

Ellie: [Still holding him] I'm sorry. But I just can't help it… I just can't.

Dane: There you go, Ellie. Now you've got me started, too.

Ellie: I'm glad you've got it in you, too.

Dane: [Separating] I guess you're not gonna want to read the book just yet.

Ellie: I'd much rather that it wait until the sun rises.

Dane placed the book and wine on the kitchen table. Ellie stood to his side, clutching her arms nervously in apprehension. Dane walked over to Ellie, kissed her and picked her up.

Dane: Upstairs…

Ellie: I don't care. But upstairs would be nicer.

Dane carried Ellie upstairs to the bedroom and placed her down upon the bed. She asked him to put on *La Traviata*. Their interlude was passionate yet gentle; their bond was firm yet tender. Their ecstasy was subdued only by the Goddess Morpheus when she caressingly carried them away into a peaceful acquiescent somber. Ellie was correct in assuming that the book could wait until later.

* * *

The sun pierced the bedroom window with the brilliance of fire. Ellie awakened and felt the cool breeze of the morning caress her brow. She turned to face Dane and discovered he wasn't there. She wondered if it hadn't all been a dream. No…his silly jester's cap was lying on the other pillow. Her fears melted away when the aroma of bacon and coffee rose up the stairway and passed through her bedroom. She heard footsteps coming upstairs, and she smiled and pretended to be still asleep.

With a kiss upon her forehead, Dane placed his fingers gingerly to her earlobe. She felt as his fingers continued to calm her body down the nape of her neck, continuing down the length of her body—around all its gentle curves, until finally reaching her toes.

Dane: You have the cutest toes I've ever seen.

Ellie: [Quietly] Don't stop…I'm still asleep. You're the most arousing alarm clock I've ever had.

Dane: Oh, really?

Ellie: You've got the job for as long as you want.

Dane: Are you hungry?

Ellie: [Turning over and holding him] Yes. Smells really good. Will it burn?

Dane: No… It's all cooked.

Ellie: So, the worst that could happen is it might get cold?

Dane: [Smiling] But we could always heat it up again…couldn't we?

Ellie: Sure. I suppose we could do that…

So, the sun was allowed to rise a little further into the morning sky.

*   *   *

After breakfast, Ellie picked up the book.

Ellie: I can't wait to read it.

Dane: It's a collection of short stories, vignettes and illustrations by yours truly. This a copy of the original.

Ellie: You've done the drawings as well?

Dane: Yes. Are you proud?

Ellie: Speechless. Honestly. I've never met a person who had his or her book published. [Smiling]

Dane: You're so cute when you try to hold back a giggle.

Ellie began to read through parts of the book.

Dane: You know, it's bad luck to begin reading someone's book before reading the dedication.

Ellie's heart jumped and began to beat swiftly and hard. *He couldn't have dedicated this to me*, she thought. *No, Ellie. You're assuming too many things, as if you were a little girl again…*

Dane: What's the matter, Ellie? Something wrong?

Ellie: Oh no… I was just thinking how special your book is going to become once all the world gets a chance to read it.

Dane: Let's just pray that half of the published copies are sold.

Ellie: If you will excuse me, nature calls. Can I bring the book with me?

Dane: Sure. It's your copy. Want some more coffee?

Ellie: Yeah. That would be great. It feels wonderful being served for a change.

Ellie returned after a few minutes, teary-eyed. Dane was just finishing pouring the coffee when he heard Ellie entering the kitchen. He turned around and looked at her with her tears.

Dane: What's the matter now? I didn't think all the stories were tragedies, and I know you couldn't have read more than two so far. . .

Ellie: Why'd you do it? You shouldn't have. I can't believe that you would've even considered it.

Dane: I love to write. I have a constant, burning desire to talking about.

Ellie: You know what I'm talking about.

Dane: The dedication? Is that it?

Ellie: [Walking over and hugging him] You're a very special man. You sure know how to make a girl feel as though she were on top of the world.

Dane: [Smelling her hair] Something comforting about these precious tears of yours rolling down my neck all the time.

Ellie released Dane and picked up the book. She read the dedication out loud.

Ellie: "For Ellie… The thorn of a rose may sting, Ah, but what a reward to be reaped! For there is not a more beautiful fragrance . . . Than that of a rose." It's beautiful, Dane.

Dane: You're the one who's beautiful.

Ellie: I don't know what to say.

Dane: Just say that you'll let me bring the manuscript to the city and publisher.

Ellie: [Smiling] Of course.

Dane: Dinner?

Ellie: Yeah.

Dane: My house at five. Don't be late. [Kissing her goodbye]

Ellie played *La Traviata* again and read Dane's stories. She found herself riding on a Ferris wheel in an amusement park on the one day of the year when it breaks down for just a minute, and you find yourself sitting next to the one you love, located right at the very top of the sky…

Ellie: Isn't this romantic?

Realizing that she was talking to herself, she glanced at Missy.

Ellie: Well, what are you looking at? [Smiling] I'm in love!

Ellie had always believed that the months of April and May were the best months. The pleasant aroma of all the budding flowers and cherry blossoms, with the combined fragrance of wet soil as it came alive, always made her senses alive. It was Ellie's definition for spring, and she always looked forward to a time when the would have someone to share it with her. Was Dane her budding spring bulb? In the months to follow, she would come to discover that a most beautiful flower would, in fact, sprout wildly and vibrantly. However, she would always have to accept the fact that the most colorful and aromatic flora live for only a short while. They dry up and fade away. The only encouraging prospect being the creation of a "good seed," one which will ensure a longer, healthier life for the plant itself.

*   *   *

It was proving to be a warm and dry spring. Ellie enjoyed walking along the beach; she usually had to walk alone, because Jeremy had always thought of it as being a waste of time. Ellie had wanted some company when she went to the shore, so she had finally adopted a puppy and named her Missy. It was last December by then, and she had given up on trying to convince Jeremy to come along, so she said the hell with him. Now it was spring again, and this time there was Dane. Would he like the beach in spring? One day in April, Ellie approached Dane on the subject.

Ellie: Do you like the beach?

Dane: I hate it! I hate the hot sand and the blazing, stroke inducing sun…and not to mention the crowds!

Ellie: [Disappointingly] Oh. That's too bad.

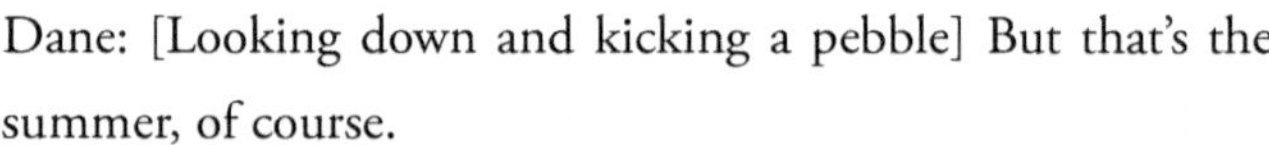

> Dane: [Looking down and kicking a pebble] But that's the summer, of course.
>
> Ellie: [Half-smiling] What?
>
> Dane: Now give me the springtime, and a girl to hold my hand, and then I'd be happy. Anybody at all, in fact, and I'd gladly kiss.

Ellie: How did you know that I loved going to the beach?

Dane: I've noticed sand around your tires in your driveway a few times.

Ellie: Ah-hah! So that's it! Do you ever…

Dane: On windy, rainy days. I used to…many times.

Ellie: You know, it's awfully windy today. Not much rain, but very windy.

Dane: You're right. It is quite windy...

Ellie: Come on! I'll drive. Let me find Missy.

After reaching the beach, they walked along the boardwalk and turned onto the sand, heading towards the water. Ellie set Missy loose and let her run around. The two meandered along the shore while Missy chased seagulls ahead, running in and out of the water in the process.

Ellie: I wonder if puppies know how to swim naturally, or if they need to learn when the time comes.

Dane: I think it's an inborn instinct. I'm not sure, though. Hasn't she ever run into deep water before?

Ellie: No… This is the first time I've set her loose so close to the water.

Dane: [Alarmed] The first time?

Ellie: Don't worry, Dane. You'll run after her and save her if she's drowning, won't you? [Looking at Dane; now getting worried]

Dane: Let's hope that we don't have to find out. Don't, Missy... You'd better not.

Ellie: I never thought of this... Oh, Missy won't... [Glancing at Missy] No! Missy! Get out of the water, NOW!

Dane: It figures. I knew it.

Ellie: Chase the seagulls on the sand...there's lots of them.

Dane: [Glancing at the one or two actually on the sand] Sure, hundreds of them.

Ellie: Christ! She's going in!

Dane: I know, I know. Here, hold these.

He handed Ellie his wallet and keys, then ran into the water, lost his footing, and fell in. He then proceeded to retrieve Missy. Three-quarters the way to her, she turned around and began to dog-paddle towards the shore. Then she stopped and began heading back into deeper water.

Dane: Missy! Is this D-Day or Bay of Pigs?!

Once reaching Missy, Dane picked her up. Standing up, Dane was in water only up to his waist and proceeded to carry her back to the shore. Once reaching the beach, Missy ran to Ellie. Dane caught up of them and wiped the salt water from his face.

Ellie: Oh, Missy... You're all wet and cold.

Dane: Hey! What about me?

Ellie: I'm sorry, Dane. Thank you for going in. I would have gone, you know.

Dane: Well, thank you for the late info. Oh, but you'll get wet, too. Don't you worry about that.

Ellie: When? [Getting suspicious] Oh, no! Dane! You wouldn't!

Dane: Who? Me? No… The pleasure is going to be all Missy's. Just about now…

As he spoke, Missy began to shake herself dry, spraying water all over Ellie. Dane watched in amusement as Ellie closed her eyes and received a good hosing-down. She had been squatting down over Missy when it happened, making it worse. Ellie got up, slowly grimacing. She didn't say a word. Finally, Dane burst out laughing uncontrollably.

Ellie: What are you laughing at! You're the one who's drenched. You must be freezing… [Then realizing] You *are* freezing. I'm sorry for getting sore at you. [Taking off her coat and then her sweater, handing the latter to Dane] Here, dry yourself off before you die of pneumonia.

Dane: [Still laughing] Put your coat back on. I'll be fine.

Dane removed his wet jacket and put on Ellie's sweater. She was laughing herself at that point.

Dane: Now, if only I can get my teeth to stop chattering, I'll be great.

Ellie: [Giggling] Had enough for one day?

Dane: Let's walk a little while longer… It's not so bad.

Dane and Ellie strolled along the boardwalk, Dane carrying his wet jacket, Ellie holding Missy by a leash. Suddenly, Missy got excited and ran free from Ellie's grip.

Ellie: Where is she going? Come back here! Missy!

They soon realized what Missy was chasing. It was a bicycle. The fat little boy all decked out in racing gear riding it meant nothing to the puppy. Upon reaching the avid cyclist, Missy began barking and trying to jump upon the bicycle, wanting to play. The overweight daredevil began to wave his hand at the dog in an attempt to scare it away. But it was of no success. Finally, the boy began to lose control of the bicycle and headed towards a concrete water fountain, near the far side of the fence of the boardwalk.

Ellie: Why is he steering towards the water fountain?

Dane: I think he's trying to ride between the fountain and the fence.

Ellie: He'll never fit. Even if the bike does, his body won't.

Dane: Don't tell me, tell him.

Dane and Ellie were running towards the scene as it/was unfolding before their eyes. Missy was ignoring their yells. Then the inevitable happened. It appeared to be a slow-motion comedy. Charlie Chaplin or Buster Keaton couldn't have choreographed it better. The youngster collided head-on into the concrete fountain with his bicycle, causing himself to tumble over, head first, up and over the handlebars, finding himself flying through the air and after a somersault, landing flat on his back. Just after hitting the floor, he flung his right arm out to his side, extending it fully. This last act was the climatic peak of the accident, for it served as a self-proclamation of lying on the spot. Like a shootout in a Western movie—"AHHH! He got me! I'm fading fast! Good-bye cruel world!" Melodramatics to the maximum.

Ellie: [Alarmed] Oh my God! He can't be!

Dane: No, I highly doubt it. [Pause] But let's get over there fast.

When only a few feet away from the sprawled-out lad, Dane saw the boy beginning to shake his head, as if to illustrate that he was waking up from the fall.

Ellie: [Concerned] Are you alright?

Boy: He bent my fork! Look! He bent my fork!

Ellie: Forget the "fork." You sure you're alright?

Boy: [Holding back tears] He bent my fork!

Dane: Let me see the bicycle…

Ellie: What's a "fork?"

Dane: These two bars coming down that hold the axle in place.

Dane showed her, then looked at the fork and spun the wheel. It spun freely and evenly. The gears were changing perfectly as well.

Dane: The fork and wheel are just fine. The gears are okay as well. Only a little scratch on your racing helmet… but that's what it's there for, you know?

Boy: I don't know. . .

Dane: Why do they have to put those fountains right there? [Pointing it out to Ellie, beginning to laugh] I mean, don't they know it's the only route for bike riders to escape from running dogs?

Ellie: [Side-mouth mumble] Stop it, Dane. [To the boy] Are you going to be able to ride?

Boy: I guess so… But I still think he bent my fork.

Dane and Ellie watched as the pudgy little racer sped away.
She looked down at Missy.

Ellie: Bad dog, Missy. What did you do? Bad dog. [Trying to be serious, she looks at Dane] He's alright, don't you think?

Dane: Why do they have to put those darn things right there?

Ellie: [Beginning to smirk] I know what you mean.

Dane: [Slowly cracking up with laughter] Did you see his face?

Ellie: [Joining in the laughter] "He bent my fork!"

Dane: [Out-of-control hilarity] It all happened as if in slow-motion!

Ellie: [Wiping tears out of eyes] This would make a great story for you.

Dane:·I can't remember the last time I laughed so hard.

Ellie: Title: "Bike Down At O.K. Coral Beach."

They went back to the car, laughing intermittingly along the way. After starting the engine, Ellie and Dane started to laugh again and continued to do so all the way home. It was a scene you had to personally witness to fully appreciate. The type of joke that sneaks up on a person when least expected…like in the subway or on elevator, when suddenly thinking about it, and one bursts out in laughter and everyone else thinks you're crazy.

*   *   *

It was a weeknight and Dane was teasing that he had news.

Ellie: Will you tell me, Dane Barringer! Tell me now, come on.

Dane: Actually, it's not really such a big thing.

Ellie: If you don't tell me, I'm… [giving the evil eye] going to leave you.

Dane: Well, since you put it that way… My agent called to tell me that the book is selling out faster than they had first thought. And better still, the publisher wants to know if I have any more short stories I'd like to publish. Do you believe that?

Ellie: That's fantastic! You did it! Do you have more stories?

Dane: Hundreds of them! . . . Well, actually, about fifty or so.

Ellie: You deserve a big hug for an award. [They embrace] Do you know what I'm gonna do for you?

Dane: [Jokingly] Get really kinky with me tonight?

Ellie: Better than that.

Dane: [Playfully] How much better could you get?

Ellie: I'm going to buy you a suit!

Dane: Oh, now… I don't know the first thing about buying a suit.

Ellie: Dane, honey, that's why I'M buying the suit.

Dane: I suppose then I'll have to get a tie, shoes, and a decent
shirt.

Ellie: I'm taking off tomorrow; we'll do it then.

Dane: Ellie…

Ellie: Yes?

Dane: [Pouting] Wouldn't you like to get a little…kinky?

Ellie: Well, if you follow me upstairs, I'll show you something my Grandma taught me.

With a wink, she took Dane by the hand and led him upstairs.

*   *   *

The following morning, Ellie took Dane to a men's store in the mall. They began browsing through the suits. Ellie held up one at a time to Dane while he considered each.

Ellie: Now HERE is a suit.

Dane: No. That's for a man like Al Capone.

Ellie: How about…THIS one?

Dane: That's Rodney Dangerfield.

Ellie: Okay… [Patiently] Let's see… [Looking] This one.

Dane: Oh, no! I shouldn't even need a reason for that one!

Ellie: Yeah. You'd probably spill tomato sauce all over it anyway. This one?

Dane: Nah, don't like the elbow patches.

Ellie: [Playfully tired out] How silly of me!

Dane: [Looking around, then picking a suit from the rack] Now, HERE's a suit! [Holding it up to himself]

Ellie: No, Dane! Please. It's so baggy.

Dane: Yeah. [To himself] Almost what a modern Hemingway would wear.

Ellie: Fine… As long as one of us is happy. Just beware of windy days. You'll look like you're wearing a toga. [Giggling]

Dane: Fine, let it all out now, while you can.

Ellie: I'm sorry. You're correct. It'll be more like you're flapping your wings, trying to fly away, but never quite leaving the ground. [Laughing] Hey, I like that idea.

Ellie purchased the suit for Dane, against her better judgement. The remainder of the day passed in a similar fashion; however, Dane allowed Ellie to pick out the shoes, while he paid for them. Next came the task of purchasing a tie, which took more time than Ellie had expected.

Ellie: You've transcended the meaning of the common-day routine of picking out even a tie,

Dane. It's usually quite a simple procedure, you know.

Dane: [Playfully] Bought many ties in your day, Ellie?

Ellie: I've had the need to buy a few.

Dane: Aren't you sorry you bothered?

Ellie: No, not yet. I'm not jumping ship until the last possible second.

Dane: Look! Now those are what I call ties. Good point.

Ellie: Where? Thank God! Anything that makes you happy.

Dane: Those strings… [Pointing as he heads towards a bolo
rack across the aisle]

Ellie: What strings?

Dane: These. [Reaching the rack] And they've all got their own stones…or are they medals?

Ellie: [Biting her lip] I suppose they are nice. And with that suit you bought, you'll need a horse to go with it.

Dane: I've always wanted a cowboy-string tie.

Ellie: They're also known as bolo ties. . . I'm sure it's time soon to come into fashion again.

Dane: Black, white, brown or green strings, Ellie? What do you think?

Ellie: [Smirking] Oh, now you need my help?

Dane: Sure I do. Why do you think I asked you to come along in the first place? [Smiling]

Suddenly, while he was choosing among colors and strings, Dane keeled over and clutched his head with his hands.

Ellie: [Giggling] What's the matter, too many decisions to make?

Dane: [In obvious pain] God!

Ellie: Dane, you're scaring the hell out of me! I don't like it.

Dane: I just can't…take any more of this.

Dane still had his hands to his head, and Ellie walked him over to the cosmetic counter and sat him down.

Ellie: [Growing more concerned] Dane, sit down and try to relax a while. Is it your head?

Dane: My head, my brain, my skull . . .

Ellie: I can take you to a doctor.

Dane: No. Maybe a glass of water and an aspirin.

Ellie: I have some. . . I'll run and get you some water. You stay here.

Dane: I'm not going anywhere, believe me.

Ellie left to get something to drink for Dane. As he sat there in agony, the girl from the cosmetic department walked up to Dane from behind the counter.

Cosmetics Girl: May I help you?

Dane: I don't believe so, unless you've got some water… It's my head.

Cosmetics Girl: Well, now, let me take a look… Don't be shy, I do this more than you may think.

Dane: [Removing his hands from his head] Really?

Cosmetics Girl: Honestly. Now let's see what we have here…

Ellie returned with a cup of soda and saw Dane talking to the cosmetician.

Ellie: [Slightly sarcastically] I see you're feeling a lot better.

Cosmetics Girl: Come and see what I've done for him.

Ellie walked up to Dane and looked at his face. She put her hand to her mouth to refrain from laughing.

Dane: Honey, what do ya think? Is it me or what!

Ellie: [Giggling] Oh, I think so. Perhaps a little violet shadowing just to enhance those pretty eyes of yours.

Dane: Stop. I think I like it just the way it is now. [To cosmetician] Thank you for all your help.

Cosmetics Girl: Very good, sir. One of each?

Dane: Each what?

Cosmetics Girl: Eye shadow, eyeliner, base makeup and blush.

Dane: [Smirking at Ellie] Right, one of each.

Cosmetics Girl: Oh, I'm so glad. I'm new at this and I wasn't sure if I did a good job.

Dane: Oh, you've done a fine job. You're a hustler, lady. That is what you are!

Cosmetics Girl: That comes to forty-five ninety-two. Will that be cash or card?

Dane: I guess I should have waited before cutting those cards like that. That will be cash. [He glances at Ellie, who's laughing lightly] I'm glad you didn't sit me down in the lingerie department.

Dane and Ellie walked slowly away from the counter. He was feeling a little light-headed.

Ellie: How's your head? Better?

Dane: Just a little dizzy now. Thanks for getting the soda.

Ellie: Dane... [Giggling]

Dane: What are you laughing at now?

Ellie: [Still laughing] Don't you think you might want to remove that makeup from your face before leaving?

Dane: Why? I might as well start getting used to wearing it. This is new to me. Anyway, I want to see if this is really twenty-four-hour makeup.

Ellie: [Looking at Dane curiously] You can't be serious?

Dane: Come on, let's go and buy a tie. [Playfully] Don't worry, you can have the lipstick.

After purchasing two bolo ties and three conventional ties, they made their way home. Dane wore his makeup well, at least for one day. Ellie took some pictures of him before he went to shower. When Dane returned downstairs, Ellie's laughing had stopped by then. He saw that Ellie had a serious expression on her face.

Dane: What's the matter, Ellie?

Ellie: What happened in the store?

Dane: I was delirious with pain and I guess she took advantage of me.

Ellie: Not that. . . I was referring to the headache.

Dane: They're nothing. They come and go every now and then…

Ellie: [Upset and angry] They're nothing? They come and go?
Christ, Dane! I thought you were going to drop dead on me!

Dane: I'm not ready to do that just yet. Dr. Jakes is going to give me stronger medicine.

Ellie: Dr. Jakes? Stronger medicine? Just how long has this been going on?

Ellie was beginning to grow concerned, and a sense of fear was rising inside her mind. She was getting a strong feeling that Dane wasn't telling her everything. Dane saw the anguish in her eyes.

Dane: Relax, Ellie. Calm down.

Ellie: [Trying not to cry] Will you tell me the truth?

Dane: I went to Dr. Jakes in the city recently for the headaches and a complete physical. He said that they're caused by nervous tension and frustration. Now that the book's done and a second one is on the way, things will let up a great deal. I'll ask him for something stronger if it happens again, just in case. And that's it in a nutshell, Ellie. So don't worry yourself silly about it.

Ellie: That's the entire truth? You sure?

Dane: Yes. I'm fine. Dr. Jakes says HE's sure, so I see no reason to doubt it.

Ellie: I'm sorry to have gotten mad with you. . .

Dane: I'm glad you care enough to get so upset. I should have told you sooner. Now give me a hug, and you can have all the makeup I bought.

Ellier: Even the blush?

Starting to smile, she gets up and walks over to Dane.

       Dane: Only if you insist.

       Ellie: I do. [Embracing him tightly] You'll tell me when you're ready. Until then, I'll just have to wait and pray.

       Dane seemed to have recuperated since the episode at the mall. Although Ellie knew that he would probably hide any indication of another bad headache, she saw no visible indication of him having a relapse.

* * *

During the spring months to follow, a menagerie of events blossomed between the two. Dane wanted to do everything and anything. They would take turns deciding what they would do next. One day in Central Park, they were strolling around. They had just gotten off the carousel and headed towards the castle. Dane sat himself down abruptly upon a bench.

Dane: This is the spot!

Ellie: What spot?

Dane: Where the man in the movie talks to Jenny.

Ellie: Your Jenny?

Dane: No, the character from *A Portrait Of Jenny.* Did you ever read the book or see the movie?

Ellie: I don't think so.

Dane: He's an artist who's lost his ambition via all his struggling. He meets a little girl in this park. She came to him on several occasions at the same spot, but each time they met, Jenny had grown years older. In no time at all, she had become a young lady. It turns out that Jenny is the spirit of a young lady who had died drowning in a storm, long ago. Inspired by her, he finds courage and reason to paint again by painting her portrait while she posed for him. Upon completing her portrait, she tells him she must leave. He discovered that she was to go and die again, for her journey was completed with the finish of her portrait. He fails in an attempt to save her, but his ambition lived on. He becomes a great artist. The End.

Ellie: I'd love to see the movie.

Dane: I've only given you the gist of the story…you'll love the movie.

Ellie: Am I your inspiration, Dane?

Dane: In many ways. Maybe I might prove to be a small inspiration for you as well. I hope so. Maybe there's a twist in the story we live together?

Ellie: A twist?

Dane: It's just an idea… [Changing the subject] Let's see the castle.

They visited many museums as well that spring. Ellie loved dinosaurs, and the Museum of Natural History offered a large collection. Ellie had always been engrossed by paleontology. Her father always explained the skeletons to her—how they may have lived, their extinction and its mystery, when they roamed the Earth millions of years past—and often bought her books on them.

Ellie: Did you know that brontosaurus skeletons had the wrong skull placed on them for years by paleontologists?

Dane: Really?

Ellie: The blades along the back of the stegosaurus were probably used as a thermostat, rather than for defense.

Ellie continued her tour for Dane, who had become amazed at her knowledge. He had even begun taking notes; soon she had an audience of visitors.

Dane: You are a very intelligent young lady. I'm impressed.

Ellie: Just you wait until we get to the early mammals.

Dane: [Smiling] Can we all come along?

Ellie: Stop teasing, Dane. [Looking at the people who had gathered] The next tour will begin at three o'clock. Thank you.

Ellie took a few of the tips offered her, embarrassed but feeling good about herself. Dane was beginning to look at her with the pride of a father.

Dane: You're in a strange mood today, aren't you? But don't stop, I like it.

Later, Dane played the astronomer.

Dane: But where's my audience?

Ellie: [Teasing] Sorry, only yours truly here. There'll be other days.

One weekend, they decided to visit the Metropolitan Museum Of Art. Dane was enchanted by the Old Masters.

Dane: Ah! Giotto, Rembrandt, Van Gogh, El Greco, Verrocchio! I have returned to pay homage to you all. Da Vinci and Michelangelo! I hope to visit Italy one day again, soon… If only time permits.

Ellie: I have a strange feeling this is going to be a very interesting tour for me.

Dane: Indeed, it shall be.

Dane was a textbook of knowledge with respect to the Renaissance. From Early to High Renaissance, Ellie was dazed with his knowledge and scholarship on the subject. He seemed to go back into time, becoming transfixed with the beauty of the art. Although she didn't take notes, she became more aware of its appreciation and concepts. Perspective and reality were the key to true art, Dane explained. She would never again look upon a painting as being "pretty." Rather, a painting was a living testimonial of the artist's perception of life itself. Ellie remained speechless during his engrossing lecture. He didn't seem to be talking to her, nor to himself. He was speaking directly to the paintings and the artists involved. Ellie found herself drifting back to a time of true rebirth and skill, the *renascimento* of life itself. She saw herself strolling near the Arno River with Dane, dressed in the custom of the *tifu*… Looking over the Ponte Vecchio into clear waters, with the sun's splendor glistening upon every ripple of the waters.

Dane: There's one more painting I want to show you, Ellie.

They made their way to the Early French Impressionists.

Dane: "The Storm!"

Ellie: Lovers . . . Interrupted by the rain… It's beautiful.

Dane: It's the dream of all lovers. In the midst of ecstasy, they are interrupted by nature itself.

Ellie: Is this the fate of all love?

Dane: Indeed, Ellie. Only nature itself may cut short temporal love.

Ellie: But it does live on. It must. I know it does.

Dane: Only to those who can accept nature and life for what it really is. Life is not fair, nor is it evil. Life simply IS… And once you get that branded into your mind, nothing can come in its way… This is TRUE love.

Ellie: Plato's *Symposium*?

Dane: No! Dane and Ellie, Act Three. [Giving Ellie a big smile]

Ellie: Well, let's see if we can't take this act to lunch, because I'm starving. This was a tour of all tours for me. I feel like I've stepped into a time machine with you today. It's depressing to have to leave it behind so soon.

Dane: I know the feeling.

Their days weren't always so cerebral, in fact, the Museum of Modern Art was quite a different experience. Upon entering the museum, Ellie and Dane came face to face with two large spools of rope, the type one might find on board a ship. The cord of the rope boasted a three-inch diameter, consisting of thousands of interwoven twines. The two spools were sitting near each other in the center of the lobby floor.

Dane: Do you suppose it's a tribute to King Kong?

Ellie was caught off-guard and burst out laughing.

Ellie: Dane! Stop it. You're embarrassing me.

Dane: Just picture it. A big, lonely ape like that goes to look for them on a cold, rainy night. But they're gone! He begins to turn mighty blue and gets really pissed-off.

Ellie: [Looking around to see if anyone is listening to him] Perhaps we had better hurry up. He'll probably be back for them soon. [Giggling]

This sort of joking occurred spontaneously throughout the museum visit that day. They decided to make it a short visit and went to the Guggenheim Museum. They spiraled the pathway leading to the top, finding things which were strange but interesting.

Ellie: At least these exhibitions are clever and constructive. They all seem to have an actual function.

Dane: Hmm, I think I like this place. I'm dying to see what's making all that noise up at the top.

Ellie: You really don't know? Well, I'm not telling.

They reached the apex at the top and Dane smiled.

Ellie: Now, here is a car!

Dane: [Looking it over] I love it. And it has sound effects.

Ellie: You know, if I had a car like this one, I never would have needed your help that rainy day.

Dane: You are so right. You could never even tried to have fooled me; I would have known that the car wasn't starting by looking at it from the roof.

Ellie: You see, you would've avoided having to meet me in the first place.

Dane: The fickle finger of fate strikes again!

Ellie: Sorry, but you can't change destiny now. You're stuck with me, so you better try and make the best of it.

Dane: Well I guess I can handle it.

Ellie: You better, dearie. Now give me a kiss, court jester.

* * *

On several occasions, Ellie had mentioned to Dane that she enjoyed going horseback riding. When she was a young girl, her uncle had lived on a ranch in upstate New York. She would spend parts of her summers there and, among other things, she loved riding her uncle's horses. Her favorite was a black stallion named Dune, with a sheen so full of shine, its hair would reflect the sunlight like a mirror. Her uncle owned three other horses as well. There was Anastasia, a white mare; Tristan, a gray stallion; and Chloe, a brown mare with white patches on her face and neck.

One afternoon, Dane came knocking on Ellie's door holding a large manilla envelope. He told her he had written something special for her. He was in a hurry because he was expecting a phone call from his publisher, so he left before Ellie looked inside.

Ellie called out, thanking Dane, and went back inside and sat on her couch while opening the envelope. Inside was a plastic folder, which contained a typewritten story entitled "The Trespasser And The Lady On The Horse." Ellie cuddled up with Missy and began to read.

It was early autumn and Tristan's mind was drifting off into many tangents. The steam was coming up for the first time in his apartment in the Bronx. It seems the older the landlord is, the more steam one gets on brisk days, he mused. Tristan had writer's block for the fourth time that month, and he knew the cure: take a drive in the Jeep and pick roads at random as you travel along. Then, park somewhere in the countryside with a bottle of wine and cheese and grow inspired. Today, his excursion would be New Jersey. Once over the Washington Bridge, he would pick routes and roads at whim and drive for a few hours.

It was close to ten in the morning when Tristan decided that the panorama was to his liking. He pulled the Jeep to the side of a dirt road and retrieved his knapsack which was filled with cheese, bread and a bottle of wine. He walked for a few minutes along the countryside and came upon a small creek. The early morning sun came screaming through the leaves of the many birch trees, and it sparkled upon the water like stars tap dancing in the sky.

Tristan sat upon a rock near the creek and opened the knapsack. Midway through his meal and the bottle of wine, he heard the distinct sounds of hoof beats coming from behind him. He grew slightly disappointed about the fact that his solitude was being interrupted. He stood and walked in the direction of the galloping animal. Just ahead of Tristan was a small kelly-green knoll, and he made his way to the top. There he stopped and observed a person riding a shining black horse, whose sheen was so pronounced, it resembled a mirror.

The rider took notice of Tristan and stopped for a few seconds. After turning the horse towards where Tristan was standing, the rider trotted towards him. As the person neared, Tristan thought it was a young man. But when they were ten yards apart, Tristan thought otherwise. Too pretty a face to be a guy, Tristan considered to himself.

"Hello!" Tristan shouted. "How are…"

But he was interrupted by the rider. "Are you lost?" inquired the young lady coldly.

"No, not really. I was just having some lunch."

"Do you realize that this is private property?" Her voice was still stern; however, there was a tinge of amity mixed in.

"I'm sorry, I didn't know. I came here to write. Is this your land?"

"My family's estate." She rode the horse up to Tristan and peered down at him.

Noticing how attractive the girl was, he inadvertently said, "Beautiful."

"Excuse me?" she tartly remarked.

Covering up his statement, Tristan said, "The land…it's absolutely beautiful."

"Oh, thank you," replied the young lady with a smirk on her face. She studied the young man. She appeared slightly apprehensive about the situation of having a stranger around. Then she asked, "Is that your jeep parked down the road?"

"Yes," Tristan replied.

"Well, it's nice that you at least had the courtesy not to drive on the landscape." Her tone had mellowed out.

"Does that mean I may stay a while longer?"

"I suppose so." She smiled and dismounted. She walked up to Tristan and removed her right-hand glove and extended her arm. "I'm Anastasia."

The girl was more beautiful than he had first perceived…she was absolutely stunning. Her sassy, lustrous hair and bright wide brown eyes were captivating. Such a simple and refined lady, dressed in a flowery blouse, jeans and boots, thought Tristan. Tristan was so caught up with her appearance, he didn't think to shake her hand.

"Hello?" she said in a curious tone.

Breaking off from his staring, and turning red with embarrassment, Tristan shook her hand and said, "I'm sorry. I'm Tristan."

"Nice to meet you." Anastasia was grinning.

"Free-living spirit," said Tristan.

"What?"

"Your name, 'Anastasia,' means: 'free-living spirit' or something to that effect."

"Well, does 'Tristan' translate into anything special?" she asked.

"Appropriately, it means 'confusion,' something like that."

"Your parents named you well," remarked Anastasia with a polite chuckle.

"Say, would you like some lunch?" asked Tristan. His desire for solitude seemed to have been pushed aside.

"Let's see what you have," replied Anastasia. She walked with Dune, her horse, to where Tristan had been previously sitting. Observing the creek, she said, "Of all the spots on this property, I can't believe you've picked my one favorite of all! It's amazing."

"I'd give anything to live around here," remarked Tristan. Then, when he looked down at the food, to his disgust he observed that it was under invasion by thousands of ants.

Noticing Tristan's dismay, Anastasia laughed and announced, "Well, I see that you've learned your first lesson about eating out in the countryside."

"Ahh! But they don't seem to like wine!" exclaimed Tristan. "Would you like a cupful?"

"Sure, why not?"

Tristan poured some wine into a cup and threw the spoiled food into a plastic bag.

"If you're still hungry, there's a little store about a mile down the road," mentioned Anastasia.

"Can I buy you some lunch?"

"We'll go Dutch. Do you know how to ride?" she asked.

"I've gone riding a half-dozen times in my life, if that means anything."

"Good enough." Anastasia seemed somewhat excited. She added, "You stay here, and I'll be back in a few minutes."

"Fine," replied Tristan.

Anastasia took the plastic bag and mounted her mare. "Just a few minutes!" she yelled as she rode away.

Tristan finished the wine and began to grow apprehensive. Great! She's going to get the sheriff or something, *he thought to himself. His insecurity got the best of him, and he decided to go back to the Jeep and leave. As he proceeded to the Jeep, he mumbled,* "She seemed like such a nice person."

As he opened the door of the Jeep, he heard Anastasia calling out to him from behind. He also heard the trotting of two horses. "I knew it!" *he said to himself.* "She's come back with someone." *He turned around and saw that there were indeed two horses; however, to his surprise, there was only one rider. Anastasia was riding the black mare, while to her side, led by the reins, was a spotted brown and white horse.* What a jerk I am! *he thought.*

As Anastasia approached him, Tristan smiled shamefully. Looking down upon Tristan, Anastasia sarcastically remarked, "Wonderful! You're the stranger on my land and it's YOU who doesn't trust ME!" *She seemed disgusted and slightly hurt.*

"Anastasia," *began Tristan.*

However, cutting him off, she exclaimed, "What were you thinking? Did you really think I was out fetching a posse so we could lynch you for trespassing?"

"But I WAS trespassing, and I don't have a right to be here. I'm sorry. I guess I was wrong about you, Anastasia. I'm really sorry."

"Lots of luck with your writing!" *she exclaimed with disgust in her voice. Then she turned to ride off.*

Tristan immediately yelled, "Anastasia! please wait! Don't go! I wouldn't know how to get back home, anyway!"

Anastasia stopped and turned the horses around again. "Do you still want to buy me lunch?" *she asked.*

"Sure," *replied Tristan, feeling relieved.*

"Okay, get on Chloe."

"Great!" he replied. After attempting three times to mount the spotted mare, Tristan finally succeeded.

"Tristan, meet Dune," she said, referring to her horse. Then, "Dune, meet the untrusting Tristan... And Chloe, you be gentle, okay? He's a beginner."

"How many horses do you own?" asked Tristan.

"Only these two," she replied. "C'mon, let's go! I hope you brought enough money. I'm hungry!"

"Hey! I thought we were going Dutch!" said Tristan with a laugh.

"Not after this!" With that, Anastasia bolted off into a gallop.

Tristan tried to catch up and finally did, but only after Anastasia had slowed down to a trot. They purchased sandwiches and a few beers and rode back to the creek. Sitting in the shade of the birch trees, they ate and talked. At one point, Tristan asked, "Do you run the ranch here for your parents?"

Bursting out with a laugh, Anastasia said, "Me?! Never! I think you've got me all wrong. I live in Manhattan. I come here every other weekend to see to my horses."

Taken back a little, Tristan asked, "What do you do for a living?"

"You'll never believe it," she replied, "I'm in sales."

"I never would have guessed," he remarked. Tristan found himself feeling pleased about the fact that Anastasia lived in Manhattan, not far away from where he lived in the Bronx.

"Are you disappointed?" she asked.

"No. Just a little surprised, though."

"Besides trying to get your stories published, what else do you do?"

"I publish poems; work as a buyer for a mail order firm; paint houses and do carpentry work,"
he replied.

"Pretty busy guy," she said with a nod of her head.

"I get bored very easily. But, when I'm inspired, I write. When I'm having a problem with a
story, I drive off in my Jeep and find a place to stop at random. Today's excursion took me way
out to New Jersey."

After eating, Anastasia and Tristan traversed the countryside on horseback. She showed him her
other favorite niches of the estate: the hills, streams, and lakes. The landscape was enormous and
well-tended.

Tristan asked, "Did you grow up here?"

"For the first twenty years of my life," she began. "After moving to the city, this land and my two
horses have been my ever-constant fortification."

"It must be all this fresh air which keeps you so beautiful and fit."

"Do you always flatter all the girls you meet?" she asked.

"Not at all. I'm a writer at heart...a short-story writer, so I have
learned to never waste words."

"Then thanks for the compliment," she replied with a smile.

"Are you married or involved with anyone?" asked Tristan.

"Not married, anyway. Does it matter?" she teased.

"I'm not sure, but, if you were married, that would be the end to all of this."

"The end to what?" she asked, continuing to tease.

"Never mind. It's getting late. Maybe you could show me on a map how to get back to New York—I have one in the Jeep." He seemed to be upset with himself.

"I'm sorry if I've teased you too much. I have a boyfriend, but nothing much of a real relationship, though."

Tristan looked up at the sky and said, almost rhetorically, "Why do you tug on my heart so?"

Anastasia looked at Tristan while he was still staring up at the vast sky. She walked up to him and took his hand and said, "Why don't you write me a story? Then you can deliver it to me in person the next time you're in Manhattan. I wouldn't mind seeing you again." She spoke her words in a soft and sincere tone.

Tristan turned and looked at her. "I would like that very much, Anastasia."

They trotted back to the jeep. Anastasia gave him the directions on how to get back to his home in the Bronx. She also gave him her Manhattan address. "I'm glad you trespassed upon my land, Tristan," said Anastasia. "I'm sorry if you didn't get to write."

Tristan smiled. "You have given me enough inspiration to fill several short stories. Thank you, Anastasia." Tristan kissed Anastasia on her cheek and bid her farewell.

She gave him a hug before he got into the Jeep. She watched as Tristan drove away. Her horse, Dune, gave a loud snort. Anastasia gave him a gentle pat and said, "You liked him, didn't you?" When Tristan was out of sight, she thought, I wonder if he likes cats?

It was ten o'clock by the time Tristan arrived home. He opened the door and saw his three cats sitting before him. They were hungry. Picking up one of the two kittens, Tristan announced, "Well, now, boy do I have a story to tell YOU!"

The End

Ellie finished reading the story Dane had written for her, wiped tears away from her eyes and leaned back upon the arm of the couch. She closed her eyes and began to think back to when she was at her uncle's ranch. She envisioned Dane being there with her all those very special summers. She saw herself riding Dune again, while Dane was galloping by her side riding Chloe.

Ellie finally knew, deep within her heart, that Dane did indeed love her.

*   *   *

The spring was passing sweetly for Dane and Ellie. It was late May, and Ellie wanted to take Dane to the botanical gardens. They brought sandwiches and fruit and a bottle of trebbiano and had just finished eating. While they were enjoying the wine and the cool breeze which was flowing through the air, Ellie began reminiscing.

Ellie: When I was a little girl, my father used to bring me here in the late spring. The colors of the spring flowers were at their peak of radiance and beauty by that time of year. And whenever a breeze came, their fragrances created an exhilarating bouquet throughout the air. [Stopping]

Dane: Go on. I'd like to hear about it.

Ellie: For me, my father was the only thing in the world that made any sense. He often sat on this bench and would place me on his knee and tell me tales of the garden elves who rode upon unicorns as they made their way around the flower beds. It was the magical touch of the elves which would allow the bulbs to begin blossoming. If the spring was too cold, the elves couldn't pierce the unthawed earth to reach the bulbs, so the flowers would come later when the ground was warmer and softer. He must have known that I didn't really believe all his stories but was correct in assuming that the fantasy of his tales inspired me deeply. A means by which I could find some harmony in times of turmoil and despair. My mother died a few years before when I was only seven. Father told of how much she loved these gardens and that her soul would return every spring and fill the air with beautiful aromas… It's strange, but that's the part of his tales which I came to believe the most… I wanted to, and a part of me still does. Then father died, just three years ago. And I was alone in the world. Jeremy came when I was at a very low point in my life. That's all academic now. And, here, today, I am with you. Don't ever leave me, Dane. I wish that every day could be as this one… beautiful sunshine, filled with tranquil fragrances, and most of all, filled with you.

Dane: You are a natural poet, Ellie. [Tears appearing] Your mother and father never left you, and neither will I. You must believe that.

Ellie: I expect you to be here in body for a long time first.

Dane was growing extremely upset and Ellie became aware of it. He was staring at the ground.

Ellie: What's the matter?

Dane: I don't ever want you to get hurt.

> Ellie: And you never shall, I know it.
>
> Dane: You must allow yourself to grow strong through your love for a person. It's that very strength which enables you to endure all obstacles.
>
> Ellie: [Concerned] Why are you talking like this?
>
> Dane: I'm sorry. It must be the wine. You know my moods.

Ellie: I believe we have a rare and very special relationship. So carefree on the one hand, and so deep and complex on the other. It's a wonderful balance, don't you think?

Dane: Come on, let's go and see if we can't find ourselves a unicorn.

Ellie and Dane got up and began to stroll the paths of the garden. Ellie knew that Dane was hiding something from her but continued to block it out from her curiosity.

The following day, they went to the zoo. They entered the Ape House.

Dane: I've always been enticed by the monkeys. They're so human-like. Looking into their eyes and facial expressions, I can almost hear them speaking to me... "We know all about it. Cornelius and Zira are real. They live! Listen to their disciples...all of us. Do not pre-judge! Do not presume!"

Ellie: [Smiling] Are you telling another story, or are you a little drunk?

Dane: Drunk with thought. Do you think I'm crazy?

Ellie: Of course not. Actually, I look forward to your tangents.

Dane: When I was a kid, I used to imagine having these conversations with the monkeys and apes. [Pointing] Look at that gibbon with her baby. She's so much like a human when she grooms her child. She'll always know where her infant is. Always.

Ellie: [Excited] Dane! I know what I can do.

Dane: [Smiling] About babies?

Ellie: Something like that...

Ellie explained how she often had to look into a family or person's background when researching into a child's past. She dealt with a Sergeant Phillips frequently who accessed information for her all the time. From orphanages to hospitals, Sgt. Phillips usually was able to discover some history of a parent or a child. She could inquire into Jenny and/or a child born to her.

Ellie: All I need from you, Dane, are some dates, descriptions…

Dane: Ellie, stop it. Don't you think I've thought of that already? Maybe I don't really want to know anymore. I could have done all that before I met you as well.

Ellie: But I would do all the researching myself… You won't have to do anything…

Dane: No. Thank you, but NO.

Ellie: But I know that you really need to know.

Dane: [Angrily] You DON'T know!

Ellie: I don't understand. . .

Dane: Don't worry… No one else ever did either. Please, Ellie, let's just drop it. Okay?

Ellie: [Dejected and upset] Fine… If that's how you want it.

Dane: Thank you anyway, but that's how I really want it.

Ellie walked away and stared through the glass of the chimpanzee case. Dane approached her from behind and placed his hand on her shoulder. Ellie didn't turn to face him.

Dane: I'm sorry. I just need some time.

Ellie: I've been giving you all the time you need. And should you ever be ready to talk about it, you let me know. I'll never bring up the subject again.

Dane: Don't be too angry with me, Ellie.

Ellie: Angry? Is that all you think it is? Just anger? What about the pain and the hurt I feel for you? It's like finding an oyster in which you KNOW there's a pearl. Only, you're not allowed to open it.

Dane: And what if it's a shattered pearl?

Ellie: I'd rather know the reality of what it truly is. Because it's only then when I can begin to deal with it.

Dane: Maybe...

Ellie: No, Dane. No maybes. Only when and if.

Dane: Do you want to go to the Bird House?

Ellie: No. I think we've had enough of the animals for today. I think I'd rather go home. [Turning around and kissing him]

Later that evening, Ellie came over and ate dinner at Dane's house. They had both calmed down and said nothing concerning what had occurred earlier. Lying next to Dane that night, Ellie stared at the ceiling.

Ellie: Is all the fun over for us, Dane?

Dane: No. I don't believe that.

They remained silent for a few minutes.

Ellie: Maybe we've gotten too close too soon... I expect too much right now. I assume there will always be certain aspects of your life I'll never know. Perhaps the same on my side. Some songs are better left unsung in public... I'm sorry if I'm such a nag at times.

Dane: You're never a nag, Ellie. I appreciate your concern, really, I do.

After a while, Dane got up and went into the bathroom. She knew he had another head-ache, but she didn't go to see. It was the third one this week. She continued staring at the ceiling, tears flowing down her cheeks. When he returned, she pretended to be asleep. She felt him slide his arm around her. It felt slightly shaky. It would be the first time he would fall asleep before her.

*   *   *

The next morning, Dane awakened alone. Ellie had gone. After getting dressed, he went to her house before she left for work. He entered her house and went into the kitchen. He could see her cup of coffee still steaming as it lay on the table. He sat himself at the table and waited. Ellie walked into the kitchen and saw Dane.

Ellie: Dane? You scared me.

Dane: Sorry. I should have knocked.

Ellie: You never have to knock on my door. You know that.

Dane: When I woke this morning, I couldn't help but leave you alone for a while with yourself…You didn't follow me into the bathroom last night.

Ellie: No. Of what help would I have been this time?

Dane: You should come see for yourself.

Ellie: Don't be morbid, Dane. Really! You think all this is a big joke?

Dane: No. Really. Please come and see.

Ellie: Now? You better not be trying to scare me.

Dane: Come tonight, after work. Okay?

Ellie: What are you up to?

Dane: It's a surprise. I'll see you later?

Ellie: I guess so.

Dane: Thanks.

He kisses her on the lips and leaves with a smile.

Ellie: Why is he so happy all of the sudden? Is he going insane?

That evening, Ellie went straight to Dane's house from work.

Ellie: Dane? Are you home? Where's my surprise?

Dane: Over here, Ellie. I'm in the bathroom.

Ellie walked into the bathroom and saw Dane near the bathtub. She placed her hands to her mouth and stared.

Ellie: Dane! It's a monkey!

Dane: Ellie, meet Zira, the squirrel-monkey of the domain.

In the bathtub, sitting on a towel, was a squirrel-monkey eating a banana.

Ellie: I can't believe it. I'd been such a silly, worried fool last night. I assumed…

Dane: That yours truly had another headache.

Ellie: Well… Yes. Dane, you're terrible! [She hugs him]

Dane: Thank you, ma'am. Now, say hello to Zira.

Ellie: Well, Hello, Zira. I just want you to know that you've got a very sick and demented friend named Dane on your hands. [Then to Dane] No more headaches? Honestly?

Dane: No more. The doctor gave me a prescription that finally works.

Ellie didn't care to know what medication the doctor had prescribed. She only cared that it worked. She didn't realize he had now resorted to his dreaded failsafe, namely morphine.

*   *   *

A few weeks later, Ellie awoke early in the morning and found that Dane wasn't in bed.

Ellie: Dane? Can't you sleep? [Noticing that the bathroom light is on] Are you alright? Another one of those headaches? Or another one of your jokes?

Ellie chose to believe the latter explanation, for he hadn't complained of any headache since the had gotten Zira. She began to smile. She got out of bed and walked into the bathroom.

Ellie: Dane… What are you up to now?

Seeing Dane, she ran to him. He was hunched over the sink while covering his eye with his hands. She could also hear his agony with the pain.

Ellie: Another headache! You're scaring the living daylights out of me!

Dane: [In distress] How the hell do you think I feel! This time it's the damned eye. I'll be fine in a minute. Please, go back to bed.

Ellie: No! I won't…I can't!

Dane: [Angry with pain] Please, Ellie! I'll be right there!

Ellie: Okay, okay. I only wanted to help.

Feeling useless and distraught, Ellie ran out of the bathroom.

Dane: [Turning around] Ellie, I'm sorry…

Dane returned to the bedroom and found Ellie lying on her stomach with her face buried in her pillow. He sat down on her side of the bed and placed his hand on her back.

Ellie: [Muffled] I only wanted to help you. Why won't you at least let me do that much for you.

Dane: Listen, Ellie. I'm going to the doctor later today. I swear to you, I will tell you exactly what he says. I promise. I can't go on lying to you any longer. I can't stand to see you this way.

Ellie: [Still under the pillow] Do you promise?

Dane: Yes.

Ellie: [Coming out from under the pillow with tears on her face] Alright. Is it better now?

Dane: Good as new.

Ellie: Come back to bed. [She holds him tightly]

Dane: I think I'd better work on the book for a while. Go back to sleep. I'll wake you for breakfast in a few hours.

After breakfast, he said he was leaving to see the doctor, and afterwards his publisher. Ellie went to her house to feed Missy. After getting there, she realized she had left her sweater at Dane's. She returned to his house and picked up the sweater. She decided to roam about the rooms for a little while. She still enjoyed looking at all the "junk" he collected. Speaking in a low voice to herself...

Ellie: [In a low voice to herself] Ah-ha! Your desk... What have you written this morning?

Picking up the pad, she noticed he had only written a single paragraph within the two hours he had been down there.

Ellie: Very lazy and sloppy this morning... Did your headache come back...or did it ever leave you in the first place?

Ellie placed the pad down and walked across to a shelf on the wall. She picked up a piece of driftwood which he said he had found on a beach in Luxor, Egypt.

Ellie: What did you say it reminded you of? "An old witch's twisted nose," that's it. [Giggling] Well, if you ask me, I think it resembles an old warlock's . . .

Just then, the phone rang. After the second ring, the answering machine picked up. She decided to let it take the message.

Receptionist: Hello Mr. Barringer, this is Dr. Engleberg's office. We're sorry, but your appointment for eleven o'clock this morning has to be postponed until Monday at the same time. Sorry for any inconvenience. Please call should there be any problem with this new date. Thank you.

Ellie began thinking about the call. *Dane said his doctor's name was Dr. Jakes. Who's this Dr. Engleberg?* She grew concerned and curious. She decided to get Dr. Engleberg's telephone number and call to find out what sort of practice he had. After getting the number, Ellie began to dial, stopped, and began again.

A JESTER FOR ELLIE

Receptionist: Hello. Doctors' Service.

Ellie: Yes, where are you located?

Receptionist: This is Sloan Kettering Hospital. We're located at…

Ellie: [Anxiously] I know where.

Receptionist: Then, how may I help you?

Ellie: Dr. Engleberg…

Receptionist: Are you inquiring about chemotherapy or radiation treatments?

Ellie: [To herself] Cancer?

Receptionist: Excuse me, are you there?

Ellie: Thank you… I must have the wrong…

Ellie dropped the phone. Not hearing anyone on the other side, the receptionist hung up. Ellie was falling into a state of shock. She sat on the floor for about an hour. She finally took notice of the off-the-hook signaling and began to come out of her mental lapse. After placing the phone back on the hook, she stood up and looked out of Dane's window. She was beginning to feel dizzy and nauseous; soon she could feel her body shaking uncontrollably.

Ellie: Got to get some fresh air, Ellie. Go outside and sit on the porch for a while. How long have you known, Dane? Before you met me… After? Is that the reason you no longer want to find out the truth about having a child? Afraid to upset the child? These treatments, Dane… just considering starting them now, or have you been getting them all along? Have they made you sterile? Dane?

She was growing more hysterical and began talking aloud.

Ellie: Dane! If possible, I'll bear you a child! Damn this world! Oh, my God!

It was late in the afternoon at that point, and Dane was walking towards Ellie.

Dane: Whose child, Ellie? Are you all right??

Ellie: Dane!

She stood up and ran to him, but just upon touching him, she stopped.

Ellie: No! You! [Becoming crazed] Why! Why have you tormented me for so long!?

Dane: Ellie… Calm down. Just relax. [Reaching out to hold her]

Ellie: [Pushing Dane away] Get off me! Don't you come near me!

Dane grabbed her and she began to beat on his chest at the onset, but soon gave in and held him tightly.

Ellie: [Distraught] Why didn't you tell me? Why?

Dane: How did you find out?

Ellie: Dr. Engleberg's service called.

Dane: I have to go back on Monday. Did they tell you everything?

Ellie: No. The words "cancer" and "chemotherapy" kind of gave it away. Is it true? Tell me. Those headaches…

Dane: I didn't know how to tell you. I didn't want to hurt you, Ellie.

Ellie: [Angrily breaking away] What did you plan to do, simply say goodbye then go off to die?! I'm SURE I would've been spared the grief by reading your obituary the day after. You're such a kind and caring soul to the ones you love. I just love short farewells.

Dane: Look, we have to talk…

Ellie: Oh, so now we have to talk! [Then, biting her lip] I'm sorry, but I really can't talk right now. I just don't have it in me; I wouldn't comprehend a single word because of the way I'm feeling right now. Maybe this is the brief farewell you've been hoping for. Perhaps not as clean-cut as you may had planned it, but mission accomplished.

Ellie had begun to turn around towards home, but she froze, facing her house.

Dane: I never meant to hurt you. At first, I tried to avoid getting involved. But I couldn't leave you. Believe it or not, I tried. You broke down all my guards. And I enjoyed giving in to you. Christ! I fell in love with you, Ellie. You may very well hate me now. I can't blame you. But in time, I believe that you'll come to accept…or possibly understand…that a relationship like ours *is* one in a million. And the good that's come out of it will be worth every shred of the pain you'll have to go through. My only regret is not telling you sooner, because in that way you would have at least been able to make a choice for yourself. I'm growing weaker by the day, Ellie. It's killing me in more ways than one. Yet, I've been trying to be strong in heart, mind and soul. It's lonely inside, and it's lonelier keeping it to myself all this time. I'm twenty-nine years old. If I had been given another thirty years, maybe I would have learned what the best way is of telling the only girl I've ever truly loved that I was dying of cancer… That the reaper deals not with time,
but rather only in bodies. [Pause] I am truly sorry to have
hurt you and put you through this torture.

Dane was drained from the emotion as well as the pain in his head. Ellie was torn and shattered. She wanted to comfort him. She had remained with her back towards Dane the whole time he had been speaking to her. She turned around but saw that he had gone inside. Ellie walked back home and looked around her rooms. Nothing made any sense anymore.

Her puppy Missy had no meaning. Her pictures and letters were mere sheets of paper. The BMW she drove every day was now only an odd-shaped clump of metal that could move on its own. She walked around in the dark when the sun went down. Lights meant nothing anymore. She was in a trance; she was irrational; she was lost. It was a night for the opera, but no music was playing that night. What was music? Nothing much more than echoes of sounds reverberating from strings, wood, metal and wind. Ellie's state of mind continued in a similar fashion for three days. She neither answered the phone nor went to work. Phones and responsibilities no longer existed. When she finally awakened from the deep sleep of her shock, it was Tuesday evening. She became conscious of being hungry and thirsty. She began trying to piece together the events of the past three days.

Ellie: Tuesday? [Listening to the radio] Where the hell did the time go? Was this all a dream?

She walked into the kitchen and found Missy eating out of the garbage, of what remained from it, anyway. Ellie snapped out of her shock fully upon seeing her puppy scavenging.

Ellie: Oh, my poor little baby. What have I done to you!? [Hugging Missy] Come on, let me feed you.

After feeding Missy, a strong sense of urgency fell upon her.

Ellie: Oh, my God! Dane!

Ellie began to cry and shake, recalling vividly the events of Saturday night just passed. She began to feel terrible for acting the way she had with him. *How can I ever face him again?* Her anger had faded, and now Ellie was feeling guilty and ashamed. She calmed herself and prepared to visit him. She first called him on the phone, but there was no answer; his answering machine was turned off as well. Ellie ran over to his house, but found no one there. She suddenly had a sickening sensation in her stomach.

Ellie: The hospital? This soon? NO! [Then in a lower voice] I can't find it in me to deal with this, but I must. If not for myself, then for Dane.

A JESTER FOR ELLIE

Ellie pulled herself together and retrieved her key to Dane's house back home, and returned to let herself in. As she stepped into his home, she began thinking about all the possibilities which might prevail. Did he die all alone? Suicide?! Moved away to be alone when it happens? There's always the hospital, of course…

Ellie walked slowly through the house, calling his name in a low, uncertain voice. She found Zira eating an apple near the bedroom window. She picked the monkey up and hugged her.

Ellie: Did you see Dane? Is he alright? Oh, how I wish Dane was right about you little guys.

Ellie thought to call the hospital. When she reached the phone, she stopped. She heard something drop by the front door. It sounded like a bell had fallen on the porch. She ran to the front door but found no one. Looking down, she did discover an envelope tied to a bell on a string. She looked around, and after seeing no one, she sat on the porch and opened the envelope. She removed a card bearing a picture of a jester holding a rose before a young maiden. Inside the card were the written words:

I was the Court's Jester
I was the Queen's clown
But today I was fired
Because I made the Princess frown.

Dearest Ellie,
Please forgive your Jester, and if you do, you may open the wine.
Love, Dane.

Sitting upon the porch, she began feeling a certain peace growing inside herself. A sense of atonement and acceptance between Dane and her. She wiped a few tears from her cheek with the back of her hand. She felt their warmth and thought of how Dane had come to find comfort in them. She smiled to herself and began talking out loud, as if knowing that Dane was near her listening.

Ellie: You said to me once that the bearing of tears makes a person real… Unashamed and proud to reveal the soul's true emotions. You were the real one, Dane. You were the one who understood that life isn't fair. It was never meant to be… Life simply IS… And once you've come to terms with it, you'll never find any false compulsion to give up.

As Ellie sat there, she heard the sound of a coin drop. Then, another, and another. She got up and discovered they were all pennies. She turned slowly and looked up to the roof. When she saw Dane, she was speechless.

Dane: Pennies from heaven.

Ellie: Dane! How long have you been up there?

Dane: All morning.

Ellie: [Not sure what to say] And you're alright?

Dane: Just having a little talk with God.

Ellie: That's nice…

Dane: Pick up the pennies. Heaven doesn't cry pennies every day, you know.

Ellie: [Cautiously] Okay. And you, in the meantime, will be coming down here, right?

Dane: Yes. I'm not crazy, Ellie.

Ellie: I know. I just want to hold you.

Dane: Shall I jump?

Ellie: No! [Concerned and alarmed at first, but then calming down] I mean, use the stairs from the attic, and I'll wait the extra minute, okay?

Dane: Fine, but don't go anywhere.

Ellie: Believe me, I won't.

After a few moments, Dane came out the front door.

Dane: You really ARE a poet, Ellie.

Ellie: It took a great inspiration to dig it out of me.

Dane: So, how have you been?

Ellie: Be quiet, Dane… Come over here.

They embraced. This time, Ellie could feel Dane's tears as they glided down her neck.

Ellie: You were right…

Dane: About what?

Ellie: Tears are extremely comforting. [Pause] I've been such a selfish fool.

They sat on the porch together under the full moon, and Dane told her everything. The cancer had been discovered two years previously; the treatments had caused the malignancy to go into remission, but had left him sterile, a small price to pay for a prolonged life. The remission lasted for two years. A few months prior to moving into the house, the cancer grew back again, and this time there was a malignancy in the brain. Thus, all the headaches. He decided to quit his job in order to finish his stories and get as many published as he could. Dr. Jakes recommended Dr. Engleberg at Sloan for better treatments. Dane explained further about finding Jenny in the hopes of learning the truth about any child of his. Being sterile, it had been his only hope. However, he had changed his mind, for he wouldn't want to hurt the child should there be one. He didn't know if he'd have the strength to hide from the child who he really was. He felt it better she live without knowing.

For Ellie, Dane's story was devastating, but there was the overbearing, more immediate part. At the onset of their meeting each other, Dane had only four to six months left. It was June now, six months later.

Dane: So, what do we do now? [Pause] I know what I should do.

Ellie: [Subdued yet definite] I'm not leaving you.

Dane: I'm not sure if that's such a good idea for you, Ellie…

Ellie: I'm still the luckiest girl in the world. You said you believed that love is a temporal thing. And so is life. Fulfillment is everlasting. I know that to be true now. I want to be there for you…I need to be there for you.

Ellie had begun to cry again. Dane attempted to console her but could not.

Ellie: You were trying to tell me for the longest time. All those little hints. How love and life aren't forever for those who cannot accept nature. All the times you spoke of not having much time to do the things you always wanted to do. The headaches… Everything was implying that you were…

Dane: Ellie, don't do this to yourself.

He embraced her and stroked her hair. Ellie was hysterical again, she couldn't hold back. After a few minutes, she calmed down and stopped crying.

Ellie: I would have your child if I could. Is there any way that the doctors might be able to…

Dane: No. It's impossible. But I've come to terms with that fact long ago. For what it's worth, I know you would be the only woman I'd want to raise a child of mine. Thank you, Ellie.

Ellie: [With a forced smile] You mentioned something about wine in the card...

Dane: Right... Michelangelo's nephew sent a case over to the house.

Ellie: I wouldn't mind having a glass or two. And Dane, I know it's late, but would you mind playing *La Traviata* for a while?

Dane: [Laughing] I've created a monster! I'd love to.

They listened to the entire opera, not speaking a single word. While making love later, Ellie found herself praying for a miracle which could never happen.

*   *   *

They promised each other not to talk about Dane's condition. Dane was used to holding it in by then; however, Ellie had to constantly force herself to refrain from bringing the matter up in conversation, out of respect for Dane. Ellie never inquired about what painkillers Dane was taking, but she knew he only took them in extreme cases. It was always apparent when he was on them, by the way and manner he spoke. Dane practically cut out using the morphine, feeling the addiction beginning to take a hold on him. Even the Percodan was beginning to scare him. He wasn't exactly sure whether it was the drugs or the tumor that was affecting his concentration on writing, but he decided that life would mean nothing to him should that become a permanent reality, if even for the last weeks of life. So Dane found himself in yet another mental conflict... pain versus loss of cognitive thought. Ellie sensed his mental anguish and feared that he might consider suicide.

Dane wrote feverishly and frequently. Ellie would leave him alone for days so as not to disturb him. Although she didn't mind allowing him time alone, she never rested in her mind until she either saw him or got a phone call from him.

Ellie: Please call me and say you're still with us. Write all you want… Don't stop. As long as I know you're alive and haven't given up, I'm satisfied, even if only hearing you typing by the window.

Ellie had taken a leave of absence from work to Dane's disapproval. She had initially said it was her vacation, but Dane knew she only pretending so. One day, they found themselves walking along the beach.

Dane: You know what I've always wanted to do?

Ellie: [Joking] Go to the moon.

Dane: Close… I've always wanted to jump from a plane.

Ellie: [Caught off-guard and worried] What!?

Dane: With a parachute, silly.

Ellie: [Relieved] Oh. That's good to hear. Will you?

Dane: No, I doubt it. Why do you think I really came down that ladder that day? Really wanting to help you with that Bimmer of yours?

Ellie: [Playfully] Oh? Then why did you come down?

Dane: I'm afraid of heights!

Ellie: Don't tease me like that.

Dane: Maybe I'll try jumping from the roof with an umbrella.

Ellie: [Concerned] Would you really?

Dane: A sensible guy like me?! You think I'm crazy or something?

Ellie: Not in a million years, dear heart.

Actually, Ellie had thought of that possibility.

*　*　*

One night a storm broke out. The wind blew hard as rain fell in a tempest. Dane was on another one of his writing streaks, this being the longest so far, four days. Thunder shook Ellie's bedroom windows loud enough to awaken her. Upon arising from bed, she had a compelling urge to look towards Dane's house. She saw that his light in his study room was on. She grew concerned.

Ellie: It's three-thirty in the morning! What you up to? Can't sleep again?

Then in the flash of the lightning, she saw him. Every muscle within her body began to twitch, and she broke out in a cold sweat.

Ellie: My God! No!

Dane was up on the roof holding an umbrella. He was un-clothed except for shorts. Ellie threw on a robe and ran out in her bare feet, across her lawn, to the street, and stopped just beneath the spot at which Dane was standing.

Ellie: Dane!

Dane: [Incoherently] Who?

Ellie: [Louder than before] Dane!

Dane: Dane's not here anymore. Dane can't think anymore… So, he left.

Ellie: Please come down here and talk to me. It's Ellie. Remember me?!

Dane: You know he's wanted to jump ever since he was twelve years old?

Ellie: Why don't you wait? I'll come up and join you!

Dane: Do you know that Leonardo Da Vinci invented the parachute?

Ellie: [Stalling for time] Did he?

Dane: But he never tried to test it.

Ellie: I suppose he knew it would work… So do you, Dane. You don't have to prove anything. [Pleading] Please, Dane. Listen to me!

After a few seconds of silence, Dane slowly came back to reality.

Dane: Ellie?

Ellie: I'm right here, Dane.

Dane: It always came easy to me. Ideas and stories have always been a part of my life. Do you know what HE did when it wouldn't come to him anymore?

Ellie suspected who Dane was referring to.

Ellie: Daniel, you are NOT Hemingway! You know a better way out. You're not a quitter. I thought you accepted and believed that nature was impartial! I believed in you when

A JESTER FOR ELLIE

you said that the human soul is stronger than her fate! Were they all lies? And what about your new novel? Are you going to let your readers down? They need another book. Do it for them. Do it for me! And most of all, do it for yourself!

Dane stared above him and into the rain. He then dropped the opened umbrella to his side.

Dane: Do you know they wanted to put me in the hospital weeks ago? But I told them I wasn't ready yet. I refused with the pride of knowing who and what I am! I wasn't ready to take hold of the Reaper's hand.

Ellie: And you were right about yourself.

Dane: I was right.

Ellie: Dane… Do you still love me?

Dane: Of course, I do.

Ellie: Do you know that I'm freezing out here?

Dane: Are you? . . . You must be.

Ellie: Yes, Dane.

Dane: I'm sorry.

Ellie: [Forcing a smile] And worse of all, do you have any idea just how silly we both look, standing out here in the rain at four in the morning!

Dane: Yeah… I guess you've got a good point. [Becoming more lucid] You know what?

Ellie: Yes. You can write a wonderful story about this.

Dane: Ellie…

Ellie: Yes, Dane.

He reached into his pocket.

Dane: One last penny from Heaven… [He throws a nickel down] Well, I guess they know about the increase in the cost of living down here. [He sits down at the edge of the roof] You know something… It's not all that unpleasant up here in the rain. Actually, it's quite peaceful…

Ellie: May I join you?

Dane: Get some blankets so you don't freeze. You'll like it up here, Ellie.

Ellie: Okay… Just don't go anywhere until I get up, alright?

Ellie ran inside, knocking over a chair in the kitchen; she grabbed some sheets off of his bed, and proceeded climbing the stairs into the attic and then up to the roof. Upon reaching the roof top, however, she didn't see Dane at the spot where he had been sitting. She became alarmed and felt terror rising inside herself.

Ellie: Dane!

Ellie ran to the edge of the roof frantically. She stopped upon reaching the edge where he had been sitting. She couldn't find the strength at first to look down, but after a few seconds she forced herself to do so. Dane wasn't there.

Dane: [From behind her] Ellie?

Ellie turned around, astounded and startled, to see Dane sitting on the other edge of the roof.

Ellie: What the...

Dane: It's not as windy … over here, Ellie.

Ellie: [Relieved] Dane! You didn't! You're here… I mean there!

Dane: Where else did you think I'd be?

Dane was talking as he normally did, as if nothing suspenseful had occurred at all. Drenched to the bone, Ellie walked over to him and placed a sheet around his shoulders. She sat herself next to him and wrapped another sheet around herself, then said the first thing on her mind.

Ellie: How is it up here?

Dane: Great. Are you okay?

Ellie: Couldn't be better. [Studying him]

Dane: You sure?

Ellie: Actually, I have no idea. I'm only glad to be sitting near you.

Dane: Would you like to hear a story?

Ellie: I'd love to.

Dane placed his arm around Ellie and told his story.

Dane: There once was a king. And this king could bear no children of his own, so the king and queen decided to adopt a little girl. She was a cute little princess, indeed. However they had a problem with this little girl. She was always depressed.

So the king offered half his kingdom to anyone who could cheer their daughter up. One day came a jester who presented himself before the king and queen, offering his services. "Once I've learned what makes the little princess pout, I shall relive her of her distress," promised the jester.

Ellie had placed her head upon Dane's shoulder by then, and had remained still and quiet throughout his tale.

Dane: The jester was led to the little girl's chamber and allowed inside alone. Upon entering, the jester sat himself down next to the princess. After a few seconds, he asked her, "Are you not happy here, little princess?"

The little girl replied, "No."

"And why not? Is this not a wonderful place to live?"

"Yes. But this means nothing to me now."

"And why not?"

"Because…"

"Because, perhaps, you feel lonely?"

"So alone, indeed! My true mother died when I was only five, yet I knew her once. However, I knew not my father. He left my mother before I was born."

"So, if you knew the identity of your true father, you would feel complete?"

"Yes, for it will be only then when I may begin my present life."

So the jester thought for a minute and replied, "Can you read?"

"Not very well."

"I have a note upon my person, written by the Squire of Beltoff."

"Why, that is where I was born!"

"Indeed? Perhaps I should read it to you."

So the jester read the note to the little princess.

"Upon the third day of April, in the year 1345, the year of our Lord, a girl was born, and given the name of Celeste, of the joined couple… Lady Angela and…"

And before the Jester could complete the sentence, the little girl interrupted him, exclaiming, "That was the name of my mother! "

"Indeed?!"

"And what of a father? Please, tell me!"

"Ahh, let's see… First, I must ask, do you believe in fact that this note refers to YOUR birth?"

"Yes, I do! Whole-heartedly, I do!"

"Very well, then, it continues as so… of the joined couple:
Lady Angela and… Jester Daniel of Beltaff."

Suddenly, the little princess grew excited and anxious, and
asked, "Are YOU my real father?"

"No, my little one. Oh…but I did know him."

"I want to cry."

"Tears of sadness?"

"No, these are tears of joy. I now know the name of my father. Please tell me, is he alive?"

"I'm sorry to say, but he died shortly after your mother. He was guilt stricken with grief. He loved your mother and he loved you, Celeste."

Then the little girl hugged the jester for telling her the truth about her true father. After their embrace, the little princess gave a wide smile to the jester. She was relieved of the burden of uncertainty of the unknown. And together the two set off to see the king and queen. Upon meeting them, the little princess ran with open arms to her new parents, smiling, and all three embraced. Afterward, the king approached the Jester and said, "Little Celeste told the queen and me of your tale and of your note. I am grateful beyond word and deed of your services. However, I once knew of a Jester of Beltaff. His name was not Daniel, nor was he known to have had a child."

"Your Highness, with all due respect, can you say you know this as fact?"

" I suppose that I do not", replied the king.

The jester released a slim grin, then said to the king, "Then, I ask you, does it really matter?"

The king agreed with the jester and added, "And, what of your reward? Anything within my power to grant you is yours."

"I do not want it. The happiness of your daughter far exceeds any material reward I can possibly receive."

So the jester left the service of the king and travelled throughout the country for the rest of his days.

Upon the completion of Dane's tale, the rain had turned into a misty drizzle. Ellie became transfixed upon the implications of the story.

Dane: I'll be finished with the book tomorrow, and then I'll check myself into the hospital.

Ellie gave him a look of sorrow and fear upon hearing the last part of his sentence.

Ellie: Hospital? [Her voice cracking] This can't be the end...

Dane: You must know it is. Look what happened tonight. I almost lost it. And quite frankly, I'm not sure just how much more of this you can take.

Ellie: I'm fine... Really, I am...

Dane: No, you're not. Look at you. You're torn apart. I don't care what happens to me at this point. At home, or in the hospital, it'll be about the same. I'm worried about your health.

Ellie: [Crying] Dane...

Dane: I love you, Ellie, for everything you're doing and going through on my behalf. It's because of you that I've decided to live to the very end. A few more days of pain for me are meaningless when compared to a person as special as yourself with a lifetime ahead of you. Believe me, it's the only way.

Ellie: [Distraught] Whatever you feel is best for you.

Dane: You know, we do look pretty silly up here in the rain like this.

Ellie: I'm glad you noticed, Dane. I'm glad you noticed.

Ellie and Dane got up and began to walk to the skylight leading to the attic.

Ellie: Was the Jester of Beltaff really the little girl's father?

Dane: I'm not sure, Ellie. Perhaps it really didn't matter.

Ellie: Perhaps.

*　*　*

The following morning was cool, fresh, and filled with sunshine. Dane had finished his novel and had the publisher send a messenger to pick it up at the house. Dane dedicated the book as follows:

To the children of unknown parents

He entitled the book *A Jester For Ellie.* It was an elaborate collection of short stories using many events from the days spent with Ellie. It was to become a bestseller after only three months. Dane would have been proud to find that he had many avid readers, and that they would benefit from his desire to continue living.

Ellie drove Dane to the hospital on that evening. He was fatigued and exhausted. During their ride, Dane told her that he was beyond any conception of pain and that he was feeling good about the finishing of his book. Ellie knew he was delirious at that point in time; she remained strong before him. After Dane was placed in a room, Ellie stayed by his side in a chair, day-in and day-out. One the third day, while she was asleep in his room, a nurse awakened her.

Nurse: Ellie… Ellie. Please wake up…

Ellie: [Waking up] What… No! He's got to hold out! Make him hold on…

Nurse: Ellie… He's still with us. Calm down…

Ellie: What's happened?

Nurse: You have a phone call. He said it's urgent. You can take the call at the nurses' desk.

Ellie: Will you stay here with Dane? Please, for just a minute.

Nurse: Don't worry. I'll be here.

Ellie ran out and talked to the caller. After hanging up the phone, she reentered Dane's room and told the nurse she had to leave. It was two in the morning, and she probably wouldn't be back until sunrise. The nurse assured Ellie that someone would check in on him every half-hour. Ellie then went to Dane who was still asleep and took him by the hand.

Ellie: Just hold on, Dane. I have to leave you for a short while, but I'll be back real soon. [Kissing him]

It was seven in the morning when she returned to Dane's room. He was still sleeping.

Ellie: Dane? I'm back. Can you hear me?

Dane: Ellie? [Slowly awakening, but semi-conscious] I guess I'm still here.

Ellie was feeling extremely nervous and couldn't find any words.

Dane: Ellie… Are you really here, or am I dreaming?

Ellie: Yes, it's really me.

Dane: It's so dark… could you open the blinds?

Turning around, she saw that the blinds were fully opened.
She held Dane's hand.

Dane: They are opened, aren't they?

Ellie: Yes.

Dane: My God, am I to go blind, too? Not that, please, not that. [Disgustedly] I'm more scared of the dark than I am of the pain.

Ellie: Maybe it will pass. Can you see me at all?

Dane: You are the most beautiful blur I've ever seen. Do you think it might pass in a few months? [Slight laugh] But don't they know I've only days left.

Ellie: Don't talk like that, honey, please.

Dane: I wanted to tell you that it's not so bad dying. But the movies have killed the spontaneity of that statement.

Ellie didn't know if she should tell Dane at that point. She couldn't fully determine if he was delirious or exhausted. She decided that she should at least try. She braced herself and held his hand more firmly.

Ellie: Yesterday, I received a phone call from Sgt. Phillips. Do you remember who he is?

Dane: I recall your mentioning him that day at the Monkey House…

Ellie: He located a friend of yours, Dane.

Dane: I only care about you right now, Ellie. I have no real friends any… [Abruptly stopping]

    Ellie: Dane…

    Dane: Jenny? No…

    Ellie: Calm down… Dane, please, just listen to me.

    Dane: Is she coming here? I don't want to see her. She has no right to see me now! [Beginning to get extremely excited] She left me… [Crying]

Ellie: She's not coming, Dane. She didn't think she could face you. Please, honey, you're getting yourself all upset.

Ellie began to cry and embraced Dane, believing that she had made a mistake. At this point, however, how could she not go through with it?

Dane: I'm alright. I'm not angry with you.

After a minute of silence, Ellie felt Dane beginning to tremble in her arms.

Dane: [Fear in his eyes] Did she tell you? Ellie, did she tell you?

Ellie: I want you to just lay back and relax for a second. *God have mercy on me for doing this to him.*

Dane turned and faced the large window of the room and stared. His sight was slightly better. He could focus upon an object; however, there was a haze surrounding it. Ellie looked to the small window of the door, and with tears in her eyes she nodded to the on-looking nurse.

Dane: I don't think I really want to know…

Dane stopped upon hearing the door opening, didn't look towards the door. He beginning to shake again. He heard light footsteps approaching his bed. In a few seconds he could feel the presence of a body. He was afraid to look, for he knew that it wasn't Ellie. He then heard a few quiet words of an unfamiliar voice.

Danielle: Hello, sir.

Shaking harder and with uncontrollable tears, Dane turned to face his visitor. There before him stood a young girl of about four or five years of age. She had a blushing smile on her face. Dane's eyes opened wide with uncertainty and over-whelming expectations. He could barely speak due to the surge of adrenalin just released.

Dane: Who… Who are you?

Danielle: My name is Danielle, sir. I'm glad to meet you.

Dane: [Uncertainly] Danielle?

Danielle: Yes, sir. Mommy says she's a friend of yours.

Dane: [Still shaking] And what is…your mommy's…name?

Danielle: Jennifer Richardson Davis.

Dane: Richardson…

Danielle: My daddy's name is Frank Davis.

Dane stared at the little girl for a few seconds. He was trembling beyond control. He was stricken with agony and ecstasy in every bit of its meaning. Barely audible and crying, he spoke.

Dane: Oh, my dear God… You're so beautiful, Danielle… Look at you… You're adorable…

Danielle: Are you real sick, sir.?

Dane: You can call me Dane, if you like.

Danielle: Okay, sir. You're a very nice man. Does it hurt? Is that why you're crying?

Dane: Oh, it hurts, Danielle. But I think it's more of a good hurt than bad right now.

Danielle: Is it like when Mommy cries when she comes home and sees me after being away a long time?

Dane: Something like that.

Danielle: Oh, then I understand.

Ellie was standing to the side, by the large window by then, listening quietly and crying. Her tears, also, were mostly "good" tears. She was still unsure about her decision. She could feel anguish. She knew that he wasn't going to tell the little girl who he really was, because it would unfairly confuse the child. Ellie also wondered whether or not Dane actually believed that this little girl was in fact his daughter. She would never know the answer to that question.

Dane: How old are you, Danielle?

Danielle: Four and a half, going on five soon.

Dane: You're getting so big. I wish I… [Abruptly stops]

Danielle: Mommy read me some of your stories. You're a good writer. When I learn more, I want to read all your stories.

Dane: I'll remember that. I'm glad you like them.

Danielle smiled at Dane. She placed her hand on his chest.

Danielle: Please don't cry…Dane. Don't worry, it will be all better real soon. Then you can come and visit us in Florida. I'll take you to the beach.

Dane: Yes, yes… Oh, yes…

Dane's emotions were hitting him like a tidal wave. He was losing control of himself. Ellie saw this was beginning to be too much for him and began to walk over to him. She knew that she had to tell Danielle that it was time to leave. Dane looked at Ellie and asked her to wait another minute, and so she did. Dane took a hold on himself as best he could.

Dane: Before you leave, Danielle… Would consider doing me a great big favor? A make-believe favor?

Danielle: [Blushing] Okay.

Dane: I promise, it will make me all well again. And it's only make-believe.

Danielle: Okay.

Dane: Just one time, could you call me… Daddy? You see, I have no daughter yet, but if I did, I'd want her to be exactly like you, Danielle.

Ellie was apprehensive after he made the request; she knew he wasn't planning to tell the little girl anything that would hurt her.

Danielle: I hope you get better real soon…Daddy.

Dane: [Biting his lip] Thank you…my little girl. [Pause] I believe it's time you got on your way back home.

Ellie took Danielle's hand at that point.

Danielle: Thank you for letting me visit you.

Dane: Dear little girl, thank YOU for making me find peace, finally.

Danielle let go of Ellie's hand, turned and kissed Dane on his cheek.

Danielle: I love you…Daddy.

Dane: [Reaching out and hugging her] And I love…I love you too…more than you'll ever know, my little girl. This is the nicest game I ever played, thank you.

Danielle: You're welcome.

Ellie took Danielle's hand again and led her to the door as Dane watched. Danielle followed Ellie out and stopped to wave goodbye.

Dane stared out the window. The sun was brighter, and his blurriness was getting a little less. He was feeling peaceful and atoned with himself. He was still crying, but not as before. Ellie walked into the room shortly after.

Dane: Ellie.

Ellie: I don't know what to say.

Dane: That must have taken a hell of a lot of courage, doing that for me.

Ellie: Courage?

Dane: Feeling torn between deciding what was best for me, not knowing how I was going to react, and later watching me fall apart.

Ellie: I don't know if I made things worse for you…

Dane: Worse? You've given a man who is dying a pacified completion to his life. I'm grateful beyond words.

Ellie went to his side and placed her head upon his chest.

Ellie: I tried to be strong for you. I tried so hard, but I still couldn't do it. I'm so sorry. I just can't tell you how much I love you. I just can't accept the fact…

Dane placed his hand upon her head.

Dane: Golden hair and silver eyes… You're a living treasure. And the ironic thing about it is that YOU found ME.

Ellie: [Giggling] And it took a lot more than a hammer and chisel.

Dane: The king, the queen, the princess, and the jester. Is that what made you wonder about a child named after me? There's Daniel, Dane, and of course, Danielle… So, Jenny still cared enough to name the child after her real father.

Ellie: Dane… Maybe I should…

Dane: No, Ellie. Please don't say anything.

Ellie: Alright.

Dane: [Voice drifting] Ellie, would you… mind lying down next to me… Just for a while… I'm feeling very tired.

Ellie: [Smiling] I was hoping you'd ask. You know how shy I am.

Ellie crawled into bed and held him.

Dane: When it's…over…there's a letter I wrote and placed in your purse when you left with Danielle. Please read it. I'm afraid that my penmanship isn't exactly what it used to be… There are a few things I really need to tell you, but I can't seem to even remember my own name right now. But, it's sure to be in the letter.

Ellie: Yes, Dane.

Ellie's mind was drifting back to the days of kings, queens, princesses and court jesters. To a time when tales and words meant everything. They could destroy or soothe the constitutions of the listener. Sometimes, truth is only that which a person comes to perceive as reality. *Does* it really matter? Not to the jester. For it is his métier to ease the turmoil within the souls of all those who care, and need, to believe.

Dane: There go those warm tears of yours, sliding down my neck again. [Long pause] Such a comfort they really are, Ellie.

Ellie: Sleep, Dane. Sleep.

Those were the last words she heard Dane speak. Dane passed away that night while Ellie was sleeping by his side, in his arms.

* * *

That morning, Ellie's actions and responses were strictly automatic. She left the hospital in a solemn, almost lifeless manner. She placed all of Dane's personal belongings into the back seat of her car and drove directly to the botanical gardens. She sat herself on the same bench she used to share with Dane. She retrieved the envelope that contained Dane's letter. She cleared her wet eyes with a tissue, and said to herself, *Okay, Ellie, you can do this.* Then, she began to read.

My dearest Fair Maiden Ellie,

I first need to tell you that I have retained a lawyer. I am leaving everything to you. Not much, but, the word "everything" has a nice ring to it. I purchased the house straight out as it is, no mortgage. The deed is inside a small box that you will find in my bedroom closet, marked "Ellie." Everything is there. Checkbooks, savings account, my book rights, etc. The lawyer's card is with all that. He knows the situation, and has my will. He will be expecting your phone call, whenever you feel up to it. Use him to sell the house if you choose.

Now, on to more important matters at hand…

I moved into your small neighborhood primarily for two reasons. First, I wanted to be somewhere quiet to finish my book of short stories. And, secondly, I best can explain it as being an attempt of learning how to die. But something else happened, instead. I met you! You have made my last months and days within this world an endearing comfort. You didn't have to do it, but your kind and loving heart made you. So, instead of learning how to leave this world, I learned how to trust and love again, while still existing within it.

Oh, Zira! My God, Ellie! Zira needs to be brought back to her family at the zoo! One of the animal keepers there gave me Zira to stay with me for a little while. I have always wanted a monkey and, being that I had written a story for him to read to his two children a couple of years ago, he loaned me Zira. We both knew it would only be for a brief period of time, considering my health situation. But things happened rather more quickly than I expected. I am so very sorry to suddenly burden you with this. My mind just seems to have been rolling downhill so much sooner and faster than I was expecting! Just send her along with a bunch of bananas; that should make her family happy when she meets up with them again!

There are many stories which I have written but remain unpublished. Most of them were inspired by you, so they truly belong to you. Then there are a few stories which are merely scribbled notes on pieces of paper. Those notes were from the many times we had shared together, but I was never quite able to properly put the emotions into complete sentences. Maybe you can try to do that?! I love you, Ellie, far more than mere words can express. I'm sorry to do this, but I have to say goodbye, my love. But do not ever let me fully go away! Whenever you want to say hello, just read one of my stories, for I am forever the jester for my beloved Ellie!

With all my love and gratitude and so much more,

Dane

Another piece of paper had fallen to the ground while Ellie had been reading the letter. It was a poem, written in Dane's handwriting.

An Ode to Ellie

Her eyes were of Silver, her hair that of Gold,
Beauty's perfect balance, as the stories often told.
Without your love, my life could not be,
So filled with joy and blessed harmony.
When I grew tired and could not freely stand,
You reached out and firmly took my hand.
So, as the Seasons come each with their weather,
You and I, my love, were meant to be together.

There was a tranquilizing and soothing bouquet of fragrances flowing along the soft summer breeze. Ellie had been sitting on the bench for a few hours now. She stood up and took a deep breath. She began to meander along the flowery paths. Perhaps one of the paths would lead her to an elf riding a unicorn, she thought to herself. But what if they really didn't exist?

Oh, but as the jester once said, does it really matter?

The End